MIDLIFE LOVE AFFAIR
A LATER IN LIFE SMALL TOWN ROMANCE

PIPER SULLIVAN

Copyright © 2022 by Piper Sullivan

All rights reserved.

No part of this book may be reproduced in any form or by any electronic or mechanical means, including information storage and retrieval systems, without written permission from the author, except for the use of brief quotations in a book review.

Sign up to my Exclusive Romance Connoisseurs' Club to receive my Free Romance, Her Fake Fiancé Billionaire Boss.

CHAPTER 1
LACEY

"This makes no sense Daddy. Why won't you even consider taking the paper online?" My father owned and operated the only paper in town, the Carson Creek Daily Journal. "If you're going to retire, then you don't have to do anything to take the paper online." I knew I sounded like a petulant child, but I didn't care. This was a good idea, one I'd been pushing for the past ten years.

Graylin Gregory, or GG as almost everyone called him, simply shook his head with the self-assuredness of a stubborn old man. "People need to have a paper in their hands, Lacey. They need to feel the paper under their fingertips, the slight stain of ink from reading the paper as soon as it arrives."

I rolled my eyes at his incredibly old school way of

thinking about how people received their daily news. "Those are also drawback for many readers, as in the ones born in the age of digital news. Online news will catch readers who have never even considered a newspaper subscription, and on top of that, it will allow readers from all over the world to learn what's going on in our little corner." It was a cheesy southern beauty queen response, and I knew that, but it also happened to be the truth.

Daddy snorted derisively and patted his slightly rounded belly. "No one outside Carson Creek cares about our little corner, and that's just fine."

"No, it's not!" For someone who prided himself on being such an astute businessman, he was being incredibly obtuse about the state of the newspaper business. "Subscriptions are declining Daddy, whether you want to believe it's permanent or not, it's happening. Not to mention that most people who grow up here don't stay here, but they have family and friends here and they like to know what's going on. You know, people like Roman and Derek and Ryan." I felt my blood pressure rising and I sucked in a deep breath, refusing to let Daddy get the better of me. I shook my head at his stubborn mule routine. "Pippa had to bring in writers from outside of Carson Creek for the Dark Horse opening just to increase exposure, how do you think that reflects on us, the sole news gatherers in town?"

Daddy glanced across the bullpen in Levi's direction. Levi Branson, world famous, award-wining journalist who my daddy believed hung the moon and wrote every important word ever created. "What do you think, Levi? Online newspapers, abomination or necessity?" He was so sure Levi was on his side, but I wasn't so sure.

That didn't mean I wanted to hear the man's opinion. "Why are you asking Levi? No offense," I said to him with a half-hearted smile. "He's a writer and he won't be running things. Then again, I probably won't be running things either. My opinion doesn't seem to matter."

As usual, Daddy ignored my outburst and kept his focus on Levi's salt and pepper hair, thick and wavy when he let it grow too long. "Well? What do you think Levi?"

Levi looked up with feigned confusion, as if he hadn't heard every single word of our argument. After a long moment, he sat back in his chair and threaded his fingers behind his head. "Sometimes there's nothing better than sitting down and reading the paper."

Daddy clapped his beefy hands with a loud laugh. "See? I told ya," he crowed with great satisfaction.

"But that's a luxury, not how I consume my news from day to day."

Daddy, now alarmed, sat up straight, his fuzzy brows dipped in concern. "So you agree with Lacey?"

Levi nodded. "Absolutely. With digital options, I can

listen with text-to-audio while I drive, exercise, cook or anything else. I prefer written news to television and digital allows me to absorb content whenever I can, wherever I am." Levi sent me a look I couldn't quite decipher and really had no desire to, because the fact still remained that his opinion mattered more than mine.

The proof of that was in Daddy's careful consideration of his words, which made me madder than a wet hen. "Good point," he drawled. "I'll consider it."

I couldn't control the frustrated growl that erupted from me, though full disclosure, I didn't try very hard to control it. I was sick of this. For the past decade, no *more* than that, I put aside my own aspirations to help run a small town newspaper that was equal parts calendar and gossip rag. I did it all, and still he didn't give me an ounce of appreciation or acknowledgement.

I was very well aware that both men's gazes were solely focused on me and I didn't give a darn. I ignored them both and yanked my jacket off the back of my chair with more force than necessary, repeated the move with my purse and turned on my father. "Well Daddy you consider that while I brush up on my resume and put my house on the market while *I consider* where I'll go next." I stormed out, and not just because I was angry, because I was on the verge of saying things that I wouldn't be able to take back, or worse, doing things that might get me arrested.

I used the short walk to the diner to calm my nerves,

to remind myself that GG was my father, an old man who was well-respected in this town, and that strangling him would land me behind bars. By the time I pulled on the door to hear the soothing sound of wind chimes, my anger had subsided by half.

"Hey Lacey, tough day?" Merlina was my favorite waitress because she was good at reading moods, and generous with refills.

"Yep. Is it over yet?"

Merlina let out her signature throaty laugh, the one that had all the high school boys sitting in her section even though she was closer to forty than thirty. "Few more hours to go I'm afraid, but it's just late enough for a beer."

"You are a godsend," I told her and tapped on the photo of the amber ale on the menu I knew from memory. "Chili cheese fries with extra jalapenos and a double-thick chocolate milkshake too, please."

Merlina whistled. "Really tough day," she sighed. "Milkshake and beer coming right up."

"Thanks," I whispered even though she'd already sauntered off, leaving me alone with thoughts I didn't want to have, but had become more necessary with each passing day. The truth was that I wasn't just mad at Daddy, I was also mad at myself for making a sacrifice no one had asked me to make. Daddy was an old man, too traditional and entirely too set in his ways. Chances were always slim he'd actually put me in charge, and now with Levi around, older, wiser and male—chances were Daddy would put him in charge and expect me to teach him the ropes. That thought reignited the anger that had dissipated on the walk over to the diner. Daddy would either never retire or never put me in charge, which meant it was time to move on. Somehow.

Despite my threats to Daddy, I couldn't actually move because I had a daughter. Stevie was thirteen years old and a cheerleader. Carson Creek was the only home she'd ever known, and I didn't want to take a happy childhood away from her when I'd already deprived her of having a two-parent household. Carson Creek was my future for at least the next five years, but that didn't mean CCDJ was my only option for work.

"This seat taken?" Levi's deep voice, thick and masculine, startled me, but before I could tell him to go away, that I didn't need his pity, he'd already dropped down on the other side of the booth.

"I suppose not," I told him just as Merlina arrived with my food. "Just don't touch my food."

Levi laughed, and it was a good laugh, a solid laugh that spoke of a life full of amusement and happiness. It was loud and deep and full-throated, like Levi was a man who made sure to enjoy every single moment of his life.

"Wouldn't dream of it."

"What can I get you, handsome?" Merlina tried to hide her smirk, but she beamed down at Levi and I couldn't blame her. He was handsome and polite, with heaps of charm.

"I'll take the turkey burger with onions, peppers and cheese, and a garden salad on the side."

I snorted at his order.

"Coming right up," Merlina promised and sauntered off once again.

"Problem?"

I shook my head because I had no problem with anything. I was a woman without problems. *Sans* problems, if you will. "No, I just don't need your pity. Or your sympathy." He frowned in confusion. "You could have gotten a burger and salad at home, which means you're here because you feel as if you need to be. As if I need something. I don't."

He laughed again and I ignored the way his laughter impacted me. "I could, but I'd have to make the burger, rinse and chop the salad and all that. Also when you get to be my age, you have to think about every meal. I'd love to have fries with my burger, but I would not love to have a heart attack or any other cardiac event, thank you very much."

I rolled my eyes at his health conscious words. "You're fifty not ninety, Levi." I stared at him for a long time as a thought occurred to me. "Tell me you're not one of those types overly worried about aging or getting fat."

Levi laughed again. "You're funny, Lacey."

"Thanks," I grumbled and stabbed at my chili fries.

"I don't mind getting old, I have an issue with *feeling* old. And who wants to be fat?" He laughed again when I didn't look convinced. "You forget that my last job was pretty stressful. War zones and famine, natural disasters as well as man-made ones. It takes a toll, and I'm trying to reverse that damage."

I nodded as if I understood. Theoretically, I did understand, but I'd lived and worked in Carson Creek for nearly all of my life. How could I possibly understand? "Do you miss it?"

"The stress? Hell no. I'm finding that I'm enjoying simple things like being a grandfather, small town living and interviewing the first Miss Tennessee in history. It's different sure, but for me it's a new adventure."

"Great evasion, but that wasn't an answer."

He smiled again, this one was different and I couldn't quite figure out the meaning behind it. "I miss telling the real stories of people's lives, not just the version that's sanitized for the masses or meant to induce fear. Some of the people I've met have lived with constant war, but still they don't live in constant fear and they're quite happy with their lives."

I smiled back because he downplayed his impressive career that spanned three decades, on and off, traveling to the most devastating and heart-breaking locations in the world. He had a knack for weaving a story, and even I knew that his talent was wasted here in Carson Creek.

"Any plans to go back out into to the world?"

"No plans, no. My priority right now is Mickey." His salad arrived first and Levi dug into it, eating it without one frown or wince, as if he actually enjoyed it. *Monster.* "Don't let GG get to you. It's a test to see if you're tough enough to handle the news business."

I snorted and shook my head. "That's not it at all. He doesn't think I can do it, and lately I'm not even sure if I want to." I'd given up my chance to become like Levi, heck to even give myself a chance to see if I was capable of becoming like him, while my brothers went out and conquered the music industry. Staying here, helping Daddy keep the paper alive hadn't been enough all these years, and it never would. "It doesn't matter."

"You'd leave?" The note of surprise in his tone shouldn't have offended me, but it did.

"Why shouldn't I? He's got you now, and we both know your opinion matters more than mine."

"That's not true Lacey. He's testing you, trust me. I've seen it a thousand times with those old timers who expect everyone to be treated the way they were treated in the sixties, before Google and the internet."

"I don't know you well enough to trust you Levi, no offense. What I know is that the future I thought would have at CCDJ is not going to happen, not ever, so I have to decide if that's okay with me, or if I need to do something else."

"Lacey," he sighed and shook his head. "Don't give up."

I finished off my chili fries and smiled at Levi. "There's a difference between giving up and knowing when it's time to cut my losses. You have a better shot at becoming the next head of CCDJ than I do, which means I have no place there. Not anymore."

CHAPTER 2
LEVI

I sighed, saddened by Lacey's dejected tone. "Talk to your father Lacey. You'll feel better." She was angry, rightfully so. GG was an ogre to work for if you were his beloved daughter. He second-guessed every word she said, every story and idea, every pitch, and he made her feel as if she would never be enough to run Carson Creek Daily Journal. I'd seen it before, dozens of times, older guys who believed the hard way was the only way to learn.

"No thanks," she answered with a bitter smile before dipping her spoon in the small bowl of chili now that her fries were gone. "I've had my fill of him."

My burger arrived with a flirtatious smile from the waitress and we ate in silence for several long minutes. The silence lasted so long I wasn't sure she would say anything else to me before requesting the bill. She resented my presence at the paper, that much was clear, but it was more than the fact that GG valued my opinion. I didn't blame her for that resentment, it was almost as if that's how GG wanted it, but it was unnerving because most people liked me. Even those who didn't trust me right away, found me likable. It was part of the job, of getting people to talk.

Lacey's plate and bowl were empty and she focused on the milkshake, bright blue eyes settled on my face. "Were you really inside the palace during the coup attempt?"

I smiled because that was definitely the question of someone who admired my work. "I was. It was terrifying as hell, men armed with machine guns and machetes interrupted what had started as a bland interview about the state of the royal family. They were angry and determined, using more force than necessary to shove us into one of the many wine cellars at the bottom of the palace."

Her lips pulled into a crooked smile as she sat back, admiration burning through her gaze. "And her Royal Highness really saved y'all?"

I couldn't help the small laugh that popped out at the memory. "She was one of the first women in the country to join the military, so she was more than handy with a gun, but what no one knew was that Queen Hashmi was also a skilled martial artist. A very impressive woman over all."

Lacey sighed wistfully, and that gave me more insight into her as a woman and a journalist. "And you're really going to be satisfied here writing up wedding announcements and gossip?"

I nodded. It was a question to be expected after the exciting life I'd led.

"Writing stories about high school sports and college prospects? Community events?"

"Don't forget the write-ups for The Old Country House." Sure, it wasn't how I pictured the tail end of my career, but I also hadn't imagined a world when I would be so estranged from my daughter. "Plans change, besides it's not about the gravity of the story you tell, it's about how you tell it." I took another bite of the burger, healthy and juicy, and tried to figure out to make her understand. "Michelle needed help with Mickey so she could finish medical school and she called me, which is a miracle on its own. I wasn't around for her a lot, not even when I was physically present, and she still turned out great. This is a huge accomplishment for her and I want to do everything I can to make sure she achieves her dreams."

She flashed a genuine smile, the first one aimed at me in the month since I relocated to Carson Creek. It was a beautiful smile, stunning really, because Lacey wasn't classically beautiful. Thick blond hair hung casually around her shoulders, almond shaped blue eyes gave her a slightly exotic look against her girl next door beauty. But her bombshell curves pulled the whole package together perfectly. *Too bad she hates me.* Maybe she did hate me, but this smile was preferable to the scowl she'd reserved for me.

"You're a good father, Levi."

"Does that mean you like me now?"

She stiffened at my question. "I don't dislike you Levi. I don't know where you got that from."

"Okay so it's not dislike, but it is resentment."

Lacey sighed with frustration, and I wondered if this would be another situation in my life I would live to regret. "I don't dislike you or resent you, Levi. I think you're a very talented writer and journalist, what I resent is that you were hired without my knowledge or consent, or even my input. That's all."

That was news to me. "GG said you were too much of a fan to be objective during the interview."

"He did not!" She shot back without any real heat and a swift eyeroll. "Of course that's what he said to soothe his own conscience."

"So you're not a fan?"

That question earned me another smile. "Of course I am. You tell wonderful stories in a thought-provoking way. But that's not the only consideration."

"I get it, I really do. It's just that I would rather us be friends and allies, not enemies, and not people who simply just tolerate each other."

Lacey nodded. "That sounds nice, and I am truly

sorry if I made you feel disliked or resented, Levi. That wasn't my intention."

My arm stretched across the table. "Apology accepted." A zing of *something* snaked from her hand to mine and I pulled back, shocked at exactly what that was. *Attraction.* "To new friends."

"I like the sound of that," she said in that adorable southern twang.

One of the many alarms set on my phone rang, a reminder that I had things in my life other than work these days. "Time to get Mickey from daycare."

"Thanks for the company Levi."

"My pleasure," I told her sincerely and slid from the booth, paying both bills before I left and made my way to the ranch house that held the town's daycare facility.

It took just a few minutes before the brick building with pink siding and roof came into view. At first glance the place looked like it belonged to some eccentric woman with a flair for drama, but as I drew closer and closer, the sounds of children's laughter and squeals grew louder. After a quick sign-in at the front desk, I made my way down a narrow hall that made me feel like a giant and turned into the room that held the four to six year old kids.

"Hey Grandpa, over here!"

I scanned the room until I spotted my grandson who jumped up and down excitedly, as if that bundle of energy could be ignored. His green eyes sparkled with the kind of happiness only small children could possess. The room was so small I crossed it three strides. "Hey kiddo, did you have a good day at school?"

"Yup." He gave an exaggerated nod that made his straight blond hair fall over his eyes. "Look, we did art today. Miss Sarah says I'm a natural."

I squatted down to look at the drawing, knowing instantly that one of the two figures, the one three times larger than the other, tossing a football across green grass, was me. "Wow kiddo this is great. Excellent detail on the football."

Mickey beamed with pride and threw himself into my arms for a tight, welcoming hug. "Thank you, Grandpa."

"Think I can have that photo?"

Mickey giggled. "We're havin' a show, the paper is in my backpack."

A show? "I can't wait to hear all about it. Ready to head home?"

The little boy nodded and spent the next five and a half minutes bouncing from person to person, delivering a personal goodbye like he was the mayor of the daycare. "Okay. Ready!"

This was the best part of my day, his tiny hand in mine as he bounced and skipped beside me, recounting every single moment of his day. "And she beat me in a race, Grandpa. Girls aren't s'posed to beat boys are they?"

"If the girl is faster or stronger or simply more talented than a boy, why shouldn't she win?"

He gasped, wide green eyes stared up at me in shock. "That's what she said."

"She sounds smart too."

"I guess," he said in a half-pout as we entered Michelle's two bedroom bungalow.

Inside the house, Mickey went through his after school routine, removing important papers and homework from his backpack while I worked on an afterschool snack. It wasn't exactly how I thought I'd ever spend my days, especially once Michelle grew up, but I hadn't felt this content in a while. It was crazy, being so content doing something so mundane, when I'd spent the last thirty years in a haze of excitement and adventure.

"Is that wockamole, Grandpa?"

I turned with an amused grin. "Close. It's *guacamole*." I slowed my pronunciation to help him repeat it. "Some people just call it guac."

"Guac," he repeated the word as if testing it out on his tongue. "Guac. Guac-a-mole. Guacamole! I got it Grandpa!"

"Good job. Be sure to say it again so you don't forget it." I poured some pretzel sticks on a plate and shoved it across the table. "Gobble, gobble."

"Yummy. You're a good guac-a-mole maker Grandpa."

"Thanks. I learned how to make it the hard way in a small Mexican village years and years ago." It was nice to recall those skills to pass on to another generation.

"You've been everywhere Grandpa."

"Not quite, but lots of places." Too many places, it turned out, because I missed nearly all of my daughter's childhood and a good chunk of her adulthood. "There a lot of the world to see Mickey."

"I want to see some," he said excitedly and fell silent for a few moments while he inhaled his snack. "Will Mama be home for dinner tonight?"

"I don't know for sure, but I think she might be stuck at the hospital tonight."

"Too bad," he said sadly, softly. "She's going to miss out on dinner. What are we having?"

I couldn't help but laugh at how easily distracted kids could be, how much they ate and how singlehanded their focus could be. "It's a surprise."

"I *love* surprises. Just give me a hint, please? I'm really good at guessing."

"You want a hint? Here it is, pockets." I liked to keep Mickey on his toes, guessing and using his brain. Besides, I liked to make dishes from my travels to teach him that it was all right to step outside of his comfort zone, when he developed one anyway.

"Pockets? Like pants pockets?"

I nodded.

"I'll guess it."

"Of course you will, but while you think about it, I have a question for you. Park, story time, or football in the yard?" It was how we spent most afternoons unless there was some town-sanctioned event to attend.

Mickey tapped his jaw and thought long and hard about how he wanted to spend the next couple of hours. "Story time and then football?"

"Sounds like a plan, but what do we do first?"

"Wash our hands!"

"That's right. I'll meet you in the yard." I stood on the porch with a fantastic view, inhaled the crisp, clean air and grinned.

This was my life now, and I loved every minute of it.

CHAPTER 3
LACEY

Lacey

The long winding driveway led to the gigantic white house was aptly named, The Old Country House. It was always a sight to behold. Gleaming white with tall columns and bright red shutters on nearly a dozen windows facing the road, it was such a beautiful place to host a wedding. Since I never planned to get married again, I had to satisfy myself with glimpses of the venues for journalistic purposes.

I arrived five minutes early for the interview and Carlotta Montgomery, event planner extraordinaire, strolled out to meet me. Carlotta was always well put together, and today's outfit was no exception. The pale teal color somehow highlighted the shades of brown in her eyes and hair.

"Lacey, you're early!" She wrapped me in a hug and squeezed tight. "Excellent. How are you?"

"Good," I sighed because I wasn't ready to share my problems with the world. "You look great."

"This old thing," she said in that typical southern belle way, complete with a playful eyeroll. "Thank you, Lacey. You look good too." If that add on had come from anyone else I might have deemed it insincere, but Carlotta was as genuine as they come. "Even though you have legs made for skirts and dresses."

"Not today, Carlotta. Where is this star athlete I'm supposed to interview?"

"Lewis will be here any minute. He stopped at the diner for coffee, so maybe more like ten minutes."

I had to stifle an annoyed sigh because in Carson Creek time, a few minutes could mean half an hour. "I should have been late," I grumbled to myself. Lewis Carroll was a former Olympian who'd grown up in Nashville but had chosen to get married at The Old Country House because he was a huge fan of The Gregory Brothers.

"Nonsense. I'm glad you're early because now I can get the skinny on you and that handsome man working under you." Carlotta giggled at her own double entendre and wrapped an arm around mine.

"The skinny? What is this an old movie from the forties?" I should have known that sharing a meal with Levi wouldn't go unnoticed. "There is no skinny,

Carlotta. I got mad at Daddy and stormed out of the office and he followed to soothe my ruffled feathers."

"Well that was mighty kind of him, wasn't it?"

"Yeah, sure it was. He's a nice guy." And playing referee between me and Daddy was probably his least favorite part of the job. "It was more like a working lunch than anything else."

"Honey, that's just no good. You can't have dibs on a man that good looking and take it for granted."

I pulled back with a frown. "Who said anything about dibs?"

Carlotta's brown eyes rolled so hard I thought this might be the time they actually got stuck. "He's yours, for now. Take advantage of it before the other women in town realize he's on the market. Men like that don't wind up single in Carson Creek every day."

"No," I snorted. "Usually they move to a place like this with a wife half their age." I wasn't bitter. Nope, not even a little bit. Maybe a tad angry but that was all.

"Your ex is an idiot, plain and simple. Don't let him be the standard by which you judge all men. He is where he belongs, in the past. But this Levi character, well he isn't just handsome, is he?" I opened my mouth to answer but Carlotta kept talking. "No, he's also accomplished and has lived a very exciting life. You'll never run out of things to talk about."

"Carlotta, stop it. Please. Levi and I are friends. Just friends and collegues."

"Okay," she conceded and held her hands up between us. "I'll just say this one thing and then I'll leave it alone. Friends often make the best lovers." She motioned as if she was zipping her lips and throwing away the key.

"Sometimes friends are *just* friends." I rolled my eyes just as the front door opened and Lewis Carroll appeared, his bride-to-be Chelsea, at his side. "I have work to do, unlike some sexed up middle-aged teenager I know." Carlotta's feminine laugh sounded behind me and I couldn't help but smile.

Lewis still possessed boyish good looks and the charm that had made him a household name a decade ago. He was easy to talk to, funny and had plenty to say about life in small town Nashville. "My fiancée grew up in New York City and she always dreamed of living in a small southern town, too many romance novels," he joked. "So it was a no-brainer to move just outside of Nashville."

"Plus it's a quick drive to your Endurance Academy?"

He smiled, almost blushed as he nodded. "My mama always said that compromise with the key to a long and happy marriage, and that's just what I'm looking to have."

Oh yeah, he had charm in spades. "I'd say you're off to a good start." When Lewis asked about my own my relationship status, I used journalist's prerogative to distract him. "I hear you're a big fan of my brothers."

His blue eyes sparkled with joy. "I am. I've seen them in concert at least once a year for about ten years now, more than that when I can."

"I have a gift for you and your future wife." I handed Lewis the bag I'd put together to thank him for sitting down with me when every paper in Nashville wanted the story on the local boy who became an Olympian.

Lewis laughed when he spotted the Gregory Brothers calendar that had broken records by selling out within an hour. "I suppose this is for Chelsea?" He laughed even louder and shook his head. "She will definitely get a kick out of this."

I rolled my eyes. "They always do."

"Thank you for this, Lacey. Truly. What a nice thing to do. Now I'm really glad I sat down with you." Which I knew he'd only done because he was a Gregory Brothers fanboy. "Also it gave me a good reason to avoid the thousandth tour of the property."

My eyes widened in horror. "It's a great property, but it doesn't quite require a thousand tours for one couple."

"Right?" He shook his head. "But Chelsea wants everything to be perfect and I just want to marry her, so here we are." Exactly the sentiment of a man who actually wanted to be married.

"Good luck to you, Lewis."

"Thanks." His face lit up in that way that told me the woman of his dreams was close by. "Hey Chelsea, look what I got!" He showed off the swag, including the calendar, and watching them share a laugh, I realized Carlotta was right. I did need to move on. At least to look like I'd moved on so the whole town didn't think I was pining after my ex. We'd never looked at each other the way Chelsea and Lewis did. We didn't fit.

"This is so great," she squealed. "Thank you, Lacey! Now we can both enjoy The Gregory Brothers." Her laugh was contagious. "What's the newspaper website again? I'd love to save the interview when it goes up."

Just like that, Chelsea's words reminded me of all the problems I had shoved aside simply so I could get on with the business of day to day life. "It will be up on all social media sites and I'll make sure to tag Lewis and you, if you'd like?"

Her brows furrowed in confusion, and I felt the bile rise up in my throat because I knew what she was thinking. It's the twenty-first century and we don't have an online presence. "Yeah, sure. That would be great."

After tossing out a few half-hearted farewells, I stomped to my car, so angry I could chew up nails and spit out a barbed wire fence. How embarrassing, to have to admit that a real working newspaper didn't have a proper web presence. I was fit to be tied even after a long lunch and a long walk around the park.

The office wasn't empty when I made my way back, so there was an audience of one—Levi—for my angry steps through the bullpen and to my office, where I stayed for the next few hours editing the stories and working on the layout to send the paper to the printer. Because I worked in the nineteen-sixties. Luckily, it was all muscle memory at this point, and it didn't take much time, giving me plenty of time to look into what it would take to get the paper up and running online as well.

I made notes on things like domain names and web hosting services, search engine optimization and servers. By the time I had all the information I needed, I felt as if I could open my own online news source. "Maybe I can." It was something I hadn't considered, not seriously, but now that I had all the information to get started, maybe it was time to give it proper consideration.

But that was for another day because it was edging toward six in the evening and I needed to get home to check in with Stevie. She was old enough to stay home on her own for a few hours, but I still didn't like leaving her alone for too long. The day was long and I was mentally and physically exhausted so I grabbed my bag and jacket, and exited my office only to stifle a groan at the sight of Daddy leaning back in his chair with his feet propped up on his desk. "See you tomorrow." I picked up my pace and hurried towards the door to avoid another run-in.

I tried to anyway.

"Clocking out early?" It would be impossible to miss the admonishment in his tone and as much as I tried, I couldn't. I turned and scowled at my own daddy. "The *paper* is put to bed and at the printer so yes, I'm leaving for the day. It's not like there's a place to offer news that might happen overnight anyway."

He smacked his lips and shook his head. "It's just a question, girl."

"It's never *just* a question with you, and I'm not a girl. What's the problem Daddy?"

"No problem," he said casually. Too dang casually for my liking. "I'm just wondering if that's how you plan to run the paper when you take over."

Those last words were just what I needed to hear to remind me that I did have another option. I shrugged, working hard to appear casual. "Seeing as that is never gonna happen, I don't know why you're worrying yourself with fantasies. Good night, Daddy." Feeling good because I said what had been unspoken between us for more than a year, I walked out of the building with more energy in my step, less weight on my shoulders.

CHAPTER 4
LEVI

Levi

"Good morning!" I kept my voice purposefully light and cheerful because I never knew what kind of atmosphere I would walk into from one morning to the next. The tension between Lacey and GG was sometimes thick enough to cut through with a knife, and I didn't want to get in the middle of it. "I brought some leftovers from last night if anyone is interested."

GG just gave a curmudgeonly grunt without pulling his gaze away from the day's paper. His ritual each day was to read every word to check for errors. Specifically Lacey's errors, or those she might have missed.

"What was for dinner last night?" The question came from her office located on the back wall of the CCDJ building.

When I first got here I thought she stayed in her office to show everyone who was boss, but now I realized that she did it to keep her distance from her father. I set down my coat and notes and took the leftovers to Lacey in her office.

"Are you a picky eater Lacey?"

She looked up and her lips curled into a playful smile I'd never seen before. "I can be. What's in the bag, Levi?"

Her eyes sparkled with mirth and I laughed. "I can't believe you just *Seven*'ed me."

"Believe it mister, now show me the goods." Lacey motioned for me to sit and looked inside the cloth bag I handed her.

"What's going on? You seem different today." The lines of stress that usually lined her eyes had been smoothed out, she sat a little taller and there was less tension in the set of her shoulders.

She shrugged and opened the first container and took a deep inhale. "That smells incredible. Did you make these?"

"That depends, tell me what's going on with you today."

She sat back and smiled at me. "I've decided to stop fighting against the tide and just go with it. What are these?"

"They're called shumai, steamed dumplings." Before I could give her the list of ingredients, Lacey had opened open the dipping sauce and popped one in her mouth. "Shrimp and pork, with scallions, ginger and garlic."

"Delicious. My goodness these are so tasty. You really made these with your own hands?"

I nodded, and pursued her attempted deflection. "Does that mean you've decided to leave CCDJ?"

"Not right away, but probably eventually. Let's just say I have more options now, and that's always a good thing." Her eyes widened and she looked up at me. "Fried rice? With *fresh* vegetables?"

I nodded. "Yep. I like to expand Mickey's horizons through food and he loves it. I tell him about my time in a particular place while we cook, and it's like he's there too."

"Wow." Lacey sat back and looked at me as if she were seeing me for the first time. "You got a four year old to eat this stuff? That's impressive."

"Thanks," I laughed and shook my head. "All these compliments in one day might explode my ego if you're not careful."

Her laughter was melodic and feminine. "I've seen your resume, I'm sure your ego was already quite healthy." She reached for another dumpling with her fingers and dunked it several times into the sauce. "Besides, maybe I'm being nice for a reason."

"I wonder what that could be."

"This is good too," she said around a mouthful of rice. "I'm horrible at using these," she said and stabbed the rice with the chopsticks rather inelegantly. "Stevie, that's my daughter, is always on me about the lack of eating options in Carson Creek and my rather boring cooking choices. You think you could show me how to make something like this?"

Her words shocked me mute. "Really?"

Lacey nodded. "I know you look at this small town single mom and you probably think, wow her life and tastebuds are incredibly exotic, but that, sadly, is not the case."

I laughed at her self-deprecating words. "Way to kill the dream, Lacey."

"Right? How disappointing." She rolled her eyes playfully. "Yes, I would seriously like for you to teach me how to make something like this or this exact thing."

"No problem. I'll do it."

She froze and then blinked as if surprised at my easy acquiescence. "You will? I mean, you will! That's great! Just whip up a list of ingredients that I'll need, and I'll do all the shopping. Your place or mine?"

Her eagerness surprised me, but it shouldn't have, Lacey was nothing if not determined when she set her mind to something. "Definitely your place because dishes are the worst part of cooking."

"Oh, okay. I can handle that. I have a thirteen year old dishwasher," she joked.

"I think it would be better if we did the shopping together to make sure we get everything. When it comes to cooking certain cuisines the substitutes aren't always intuitive." I hoped I didn't offend her, but she was new to this type of cooking and I knew there was already one man in her life who second-guessed her every decision.

"Oh, um sure. That makes sense. The only soy sauce in my place are the packets from the one Chinese restaurant in town, and Stevie swears it's fake Chinese food." She laughed and took another shumai. "Bring Mickey, it'll really bruise Stevie's ego to have a toddler make better food than her."

"You are a wicked woman, Lacey Gregory."

"Maybe so, but life with a teenager is a constant battle, and sometimes you have to take your wins where you can."

The same could be said of working with family members. "Do I get to be in on your little secret?"

"Not yet. When, or if it becomes something to tell, I promise to let you in on it."

"That sounds ominous."

"Does it?" She laughed. "I've always wanted to be a bit mysterious."

"Right now you're succeeding, believe me."

"Well now you're just sucking up to me. Did Daddy tell you about the story I have for you already?"

I blinked and sat up a little taller. "No. Tell me." I couldn't hide the excitement in my voice at the idea of a real story. No matter what I told Lacey, some stories were more interesting than others.

"There's a lawyer in town, a female lawyer who moved here five years ago from Knoxville. She takes on divorce and domestic violence cases, her clients are almost exclusively women. Before she came to town the women never succeeded in court, which statistically is just unlikely. On top of that, she's been assaulted several times by angry soon-t0-be ex-husbands."

"Wow." It was right up my alley. "You sure you don't want this story?"

"No. I think you have the experience and skill to handle this how it should be handled."

Another compliment? "Thank you."

She simply smiled and suddenly I felt like a man half my age, crushing on a woman who was out of my league.

Good thing I was too old and too wise to crush on a beautiful woman who was also, technically, my boss.

CHAPTER 5
LACEY

"Do you have a husband Miss Lacey?" Mickey looked up at me with a wide smile and bottomless green eyes, waiting for my answer in the middle of the ethnic foods aisle of the supermarket.

I looked down at him with a suppressed smile and shook my head. "I don't. Do you?"

The little boy giggled and shook his head. "I'm too young, but you're not. Why don't you have a husband? Is he stupid too, like my dad?"

"Mickey," Levi turned away from the rows of dark soy sauce and attempted to admonish his grandson. "That's not nice."

He shrugged and switched his gaze to Levi. "Mama says it all the time, he's too stupid to realize he's missing out." Mickey turned back to me. "Don't you think my grandpa is handsome? Mama said all the older women in town like him. Are you an old woman too?"

Some days I felt like an old woman, like today. Too many years had passed since I was able to experience the joy and the horror of an inquisitive toddler. "Do I look old to you, Mickey?"

He stared at me for so long, adorable face twisted in deep contemplation until he had an answer. "You look younger than Grandpa, but older than Mama."

I laughed at his honesty. "Thank you, but let me offer you a little tip that you should remember for the rest of your life. Women don't like to talk about their age."

Mickey's brows dipped into a confused frown. "Why not? I can't wait 'til I'm older. I'm gonna be big and strong, and I'm gonna see the world just like Grandpa."

My heart melted and I was pretty sure I fell a little in love with the adorable boy in that moment. "Really?"

He gave an enthusiastic nod and let Levi's hand go to take mine.

"I think you'll do all that and a whole lot more." His small hand was soft and tiny in mine and I felt that pang in my chest I always felt at the thought that Stevie would be my only child, that I would never have the big, boisterous family I'd always wanted.

"I forgot to get ginger." Levi looked down at Mickey and then to me, a small smile on his lips. "I'll run and get it, plus some more scallions. Meet you in the freezer section?"

I nodded and gave Mickey a little tug. "Come on kiddo, you can show me the best ice cream to get." I winked and the sound of his little boy laughter hit me with another pang of longing.

"My favorite ice cream is the swirls. Chocolate and vanilla. Orange cream and vanilla. Moose tracks. Rocky Road. Mint chocolate chip." He skipped beside me with more energy than I could muster at the beginning of the day, never mind during early evening.

"Sounds to me like you just like having two flavors in one. Greedy boy."

Mickey flashed a devilish grin and nodded as if we were sharing some big secret. "Yeah."

Mickey kept up a running commentary as we finished up the shopping for dinner ingredients as well as a few pantry staples I'd meant to pick up for days. The little boy was such a bundle of energy that it shocked me when he settled on the sofa with a book when we got back to my place. "Great kid you have there, Levi."

"Right?" He started to unpack the grocery bags. "Sometimes I think I'm just one of those grandparents who thinks they've somehow found the greatest little kid on earth, but most days I'm pretty sure I'm right."

I laughed and shoved the milk and eggs in the fridge. "You're right about this," I assured him before I went in search of the aprons I used when it was time to perform my parental duties for bake sales and candy grams. "Here you go."

Levi frowned at the frilly apron and shook his head. "I don't need that."

My brows quirked at his offended tone. "Oh. Right. Too masculine to protect your clothes. Got it." I tied my own apron and stared down at the ingredients with a smirk. "What do we do first?"

Levi sighed and gripped the apron a little tighter when I tried to take it from him. "I'll look ridiculous."

"You'd look more ridiculous with a shirt covered in dumpling filling."

His thick bushy brows furrowed. "The filling goes *inside* the filling, but I'm beginning to see your real problem in the kitchen."

"Yeah?" I folded my arms. "What's that?"

"You think dumpling filling will end up on my shirt, so clearly you have no idea how food works."

His wry tone tore a belly laugh from me, which drew a brief moment of attention from Mickey before he turned back to his book. "You're funny."

"I know." He flashed a handsome smile, and suddenly I knew exactly what his daughter meant. Levi was handsome, charming, fit and smart. He was a catch at any age, but more so in a small town where dating options were limited.

"Modest, too."

Levi shrugged and pointed to the meat on the counter. "You want to do the meat or the vegetables?"

"Meat," I answered and we unconsciously split up the kitchen space with Levi working near the fridge and me near the sink, getting the shrimp minced up in the food processor and then dicing the pork in neat little cubes. "All done."

Levi smelled incredible as he stood beside me showing me the technique he'd learned to fold the dumplings into a perfect fan purse. He smelled like a man, a real man who kept his scent clean and masculine. I leaned in a little closer before I stopped myself. What was I doing? This guy was totally off limits. Completely. Not only was he an employee of the newspaper, he was also angling for my job.

"And that's all you have to do."

I blinked to clear my mind and smiled. "Got it."

The front door opened and I heard the distinct sound of Stevie kicking off her sneakers and hanging up one of her twelve thousand hoodies. "Mom, I'm home! Mom? Where's my mom?"

"In the kitchen," Mickey answered helpfully.

"Mom, who is this little kid...oh. You have a date? Ew."

"Gee thanks, daughter. Hold back with the compliments, why don't ya?"

Stevie's lips twitched and she crossed the kitchen to

wrap her arms around me. "I didn't mean it like that, but who are they?"

"This is Levi, he's a journalist and he's working at the paper. Mickey is his grandson."

My daughter's eyes flashed with mischief. "The one GG thinks can do no wrong?"

I laughed. "One and the same."

"Oh. Nice to meet you, I'm Stevie." My body relaxed at her good manners even if I still stung a little over her unintended slight. "You look exactly how I imagined a world traveling journalist would. Though I expected a corduroy blazer."

Levi accepted her hand with a chuckle. "It's too hot in most places for corduroy and blazers."

"Hmph, I never thought of that. Good point. What's all this?"

Levi flashed a killer smile at Stevie who beamed right back. "Shumai."

At Stevie's frown, I explained. "You're always complaining about the lack of variety in Carson Creek, so Levi was kind enough to teach me how to make shumai, which are dumplings."

"Dumplings? Seriously?" She squealed so loudly it may have started all the neighborhood dogs barking. "This is so cool! Can I help?"

"Sure. You can make the sauce," Levi told her and guided her step by step through each ingredient. "Now whisk it up until it starts to foam and set it aside. Better yet, split it so we don't have to share. Your mom is a sauce hog."

"Am not," I insisted but the effect was ruined at the knowing look he shot me. "It was really good, so that's actually a compliment to you."

"Thanks?"

"You're welcome," I sighed and went back to folding dumplings.

Dinner was fun and a little bit boisterous, exactly how I'd always wanted. Almost exactly, anyway. Stevie asked Levi a million questions about his travels, which he answered with patience and kindness, and a hint of amusement. Mickey peppered the table with bits of trivia that only little boys found impressive.

The atmosphere was loud, the food good and the company was entertaining. It was a good night. With Levi of all people. *Stranger things have happened,* I told myself and refused to feel even a little bit flattered by the appreciative look he gave me across the table.

"That was the best Chinese food I have ever had," Stevie said with a sigh and an air of authority. "I haven't had much, but this was better than anything I've ever had. Thank you, Levi Branson."

"Mr. Branson," I corrected her and was rewarded with an eyeroll for my efforts.

"It was my pleasure. I love to expand people's horizons."

"You have to try the pigeon pie," Mickey offered,

looking at Stevie with hero worship as he leaned in with a mischievous grin. "There's no pigeon in it though."

"That's weird," she offered with a frown.

"Right?" Mickey giggled. "I know."

"Anytime you need a babysitter, Mr. Branson, I will accept payment in the form of food. Nothing boring like steak and potatoes though." To punctuate her point, Stevie pointed in Levi's direction.

He held his hands up with a laugh. "I wouldn't dream of it, but I will keep your offer in mind."

"If you want to go on a date or whatever old people do together."

"Stevie!"

Levi simply laughed again. "You need to work on your compliments, Stevie."

She laughed. "Not the first time I've heard that, so you might have a point."

CHAPTER 6
LEVI

The last time I stood beside a woman, sharing the task of cleaning up after dinner, I was a married man. This time there were two kids in the living room fighting sleep instead of one. That was a lifetime ago, and it was never as easygoing as it was with Lacey. She didn't need to fill every moment of silence with mindless chatter, and when she did speak, it was with a purpose.

"You really don't need to help with the dishes. You did enough." She turned and flashed a beautiful smile up at me. "Thank you again, for the help with dinner. I owe you one."

A favor from Lacey wouldn't be so bad. "If you insist." It was meant to just be a good deed to help out a colleague, but I learned in my career that you never turn down a favor. "Now that we're friends, can I ask you about Stevie's dad?"

Lacey sighed and stared out the window into the black backyard. I didn't think she would answer, but eventually she did. "The divorce was finalized six months ago, but he's been living with the twenty-four year old love of his life for the past eighteen."

"I'm sorry."

"Don't be." Lacey shook her head to clear her mind of whatever thoughts put the sad look on her face and sighed. "I don't miss him and I don't want him back, it's just that I worry about Stevie missing out on having a traditional family unit, you know?"

"It's part of why I'm here in Carson Creek now. I chose to take every assignment offered to me when Michelle was a child, and the worst part? I knew, deep down I knew the damage it would do to my marriage and my daughter. Still, I took them because I couldn't help myself, I was so damn determined to become who I wanted to become that I didn't put anyone else first. Ever."

"Wow. No wonder you're such a good writer. You have a way with words, Levi."

"Thanks," I answered around a laugh. "I'm trying to make up for it now, not that it's even possible."

"You can't make up for what you missed, but you can give Mickey what he's missing, a male role model. A hero."

"I'm no hero," I shot back with a growl.

"Maybe not to you, but he thinks you're the best man who ever lived." She sighed again, this time it was more amused and wistful than anything. "It is nice to know that you're human like the rest of us though."

I laughed and bumped her shoulder. "Definitely human. With more flaws than the average human, I'm sure."

Lacey barked out a laugh and rolled her eyes. "So, you even demure better than the rest of us? Typical."

That comeback made me laugh, Lacey is funny and charming. Despite the hard edges around her and the way she focused on business, she was a laidback woman. She was easy to be around. "Your husband sounds like an idiot."

"Ex-husband," she corrected automatically. "Why? You don't like twenty-four year old beauty queens?"

"Who doesn't," I snorted. "They're nice to look at, but have you ever talked to a twenty-four year old at this age? It's exhausting. Even Michelle, and she's a med student." I shook my head thinking about what an old man I must sound like, complaining about *kids these days*. "With the slang and the constant social media, I feel like I'm in a different century."

Lacey's feminine laugh echoed in the kitchen. "My youngest brother is thirty-five but he's a rock star, which makes him about twenty-four in maturity, so I do know what you mean. But my ex says he loves her and he's gone, and I'm actually fine with that. Well, I'm finally fine with it now."

"The elusive growth we were warned about as kids?"

"Nope," she laughed. "After I went through my stages of grief and rage, I realized that Martin had it right. We liked each other well enough, but sharing a life with someone is too difficult, too complicated for like to be enough to get you through all the ups and downs. I'm not condoning his cheating, but he did the one thing I probably wouldn't have, filed the divorce papers."

"Stevie?"

She nodded. "Yes, I would have put up with it for another few years just to give her the childhood she deserved."

"Now you don't have to."

"Exactly." She flashed a smile that didn't quite reach her eyes. "What about you?"

"Been divorced for longer than I was married. We married too young and for all the wrong reasons. Maybe it could have worked, but my career made it impossible to try."

"You're retired now, aren't you?"

"Maybe, I am. Maybe I'm just temporarily benched for the foreseeable future."

"Won't be so temporary when Daddy offers to make you Editor-in-Chief." Her words were meant to be flippant, I could tell that much even though they came across as bitter. "Sorry."

"Don't be. I have no interest in running a newspaper, no offense. But I don't. It's too much of all the things I don't like about journalism." I wasn't cut out for administrative tasks, advertising and leading meetings. I preferred to chase the story.

"None taken. I don't enjoy it much either, but I've earned it. And if I haven't, well..." She shrugged and refused to finish whatever she'd been about to share. Lacey turned to me slowly.

I turned to face her, up close for the first time since we started working together. Her eyes were big and blue, but they were a swirl of rainbow colors. Green and gold and even some brown transformed her blue into something ethereal, stunning.

"Levi," she sighed and I saw her pulse flutter at the base of her throat, a sure sign she was turned on. Heat and appreciation darkened her eyes and I sucked in a breath.

"Lacey."

I don't know who took the first step forward, Lacey or me, all I knew was that our arms circled each other, our pulses throbbed with the heat of desire. Closer and closer until our lips almost touched.

Until a scream came from upstairs followed by hurried footsteps. "Mom. Mom, you are not going to believe it!"

Lacey took a step back, her gaze still fixed on my

face, a mix of confusion and disbelief swam in her eyes. "What is it, Stevie?"

"Uncle Roman has the number one album in the country! It's official, he's a solo success!" She squealed as if her uncle's success was her own, and I couldn't help but smile at her excitement. "I'm gonna text him," she said and rushed off.

The moment had passed and we both knew it, but I knew it would happen again, and soon. She hadn't pulled back, hadn't glared at me, and so far, she hadn't kicked me out.

"Congratulations?"

Lacey shrugged. "I'm proud of him, but it's nothing to do with me." Her lips curled into a grin. "You want an autograph?"

She was teasing I was sure. "Michelle might love it, actually. I can't say for sure."

"Find out and let me know," she said sincerely. "In the meantime, you've got a passed out little boy who should probably be sleeping in his bed."

"Of course." I knew she wasn't really kicking me out, but Lacey needed space. "I'll see you tomorrow."

"Definitely. Thanks again, Levi. I had a good time with you and Mickey."

"Yeah, me too." I had better than a good time.

Far better than I expected.

CHAPTER 7
LACEY

After my research into taking the newspaper online and my conversation with Levi, I felt better about pretty much everything. At least until I arrived at the newspaper office this morning.

"Mornin' Daddy." I breezed in like nothing was wrong, as if there was nothing on my mind, and made a beeline towards my office before Daddy could ruin my day.

"Lacey, we need to have a talk."

My feet stopped, or more like they stuttered in my haste to get to the office. A slow sigh escaped before I turned, barely able to stifle my eyeroll. "About?"

"Well," he answered slowly with a sigh of his own. "It's about that idea of yours to go online with the newspaper. We need to hold off on that for a while. A good long while."

I just nodded because there was no point trying to talk sense into my father. He was as stubborn as a mule, and determined to make my life as difficult as possible.

"Fine." I was more certain than ever that the future I'd planned on, no that I'd planned my entire life around, was slowly fading into nothing.

Into less than nothing.

It was time to make a decision. A real decision, not one made out of anger or spite or even jealousy. I just had to—finally—do what was right for me. No one else, but me. "I'm heading out to see what's going on around town. See you later."

"All right." He waved me off, already distracted by his daily ritual of combing through every line, every character of the entire paper so he could point out my mistakes later. "We'll talk about the online thing later. I promise."

"Right. Sure." It didn't matter and it wasn't worth fighting over, not anymore. I needed a sounding board, one that wasn't personally invested in the outcome of however this all turned out. Pippa would be good, but Ryan would be even better, so I headed to Dark Horse and hoped for the best.

The restaurant was mostly empty just before noon which meant Pippa would be busy prepping for the shift ahead, despite being two hundred months pregnant. "Hey Devon, is Ryan around?"

He nodded. "In the office. Go on back, I think they're

decent or at least fully clothed." Devon was my brother's assistant and he motioned me to the back of the restaurant with a smirk.

"Thank you. I think." I knew the deal with a newly reunited Pippa and Ryan, and the smart thing to do would be to knock first, and wait. But I was in no mood to wait so I barged right inside.

"Oh hey guys, glad I'm not interrupting."

To their credit, neither of them pulled apart, gasped in shock or pretended not to be caught in an intimate position. "Lacey, how is my favorite sister?"

I rolled my eyes. "Besides the fact that I'm your only sister, I'm fine. Sort of. I need to talk, so can you guys put your tongues away for a little while? Please?"

"Sure." Pippa slid from Ryan's lap and smoothed her blouse with a sheepish grin. "What's up?"

"It's Daddy. He's never going to let me take over the paper and he will never ever retire, so I'm just wasting my time. He refuses to update the paper into the twenty-first century, he hired another employee without telling me and...well, I'm done. Completely and totally done." It was scary at first, thinking about it, but once I said it out loud I knew it was the right decision to make. "I think I have to leave."

"Carson Creek? You can't leave Lacey, you just... can't." She rubbed her belly, brows furrowed in pain and sadness. "You can't."

"No, not Carson Creek, just the CCDJ." I sighed

because as much as the thought of leaving town appealed, there were many reasons I couldn't. "Stevie loves it here and this would the worst time to uproot her, after the divorce and everything. But I can't stay at the paper if nothing changes." The idea of doing something else was appealing right now, and for the sake of my sanity, I had to.

Ryan hadn't said anything for a long time and I swallowed, waited for him to say something. Anything. "You love being a journalist."

"I've always wanted to be a journalist but I'm not, I'm not even close to one. I'm like a court reporter, or a gossip columnist. I don't dig up dirt or stories or get scoops on anything."

"I thought you were happy here?" I understood his confusion because I'd never said anything to my brothers, never voiced any concern or complaint about my job.

"I was, or at least I was planning on being happy here because I thought after I put in my time, did what Daddy wanted, that I'd get what I wanted. But it's becoming increasingly clear that it's never going to happen. I'm never going to get a say over what the paper publishes, or how it's published. So, I need to find a way to be happy. Right?" No one said anything and I started to feel foolish. "Right?"

Ryan said nothing and I could only imagine what was going on in his head. Pippa laid her hand on top of mine, sympathy filled her face. "If that's what you need to do Lacey, we support you. Totally." She looked to Ryan. "Right honey?" The look she gave my brother warned him against whatever he was building up to say, but it didn't work.

Ryan was nothing, if not blunt. "You can't leave Daddy."

I folded my arms across my chest. "And why the hell not? Are you and Derek and Roman the only ones allowed to go out and live your dreams? I'm supposed to stay here and take care of the cantankerous old man."

"That cantankerous old man is your father," he roared.

"Yeah well, he's yours too, and that didn't make you stick around, not any of you." Ryan's words made me angry, no that's not right, they pissed me off. "I stayed here and worked with Daddy while you traveled the world and got rich. What did I get? Divorced and stuck in a career that's going nowhere. That's going to change, whether you like it or not."

"Yeah, and what's Daddy supposed to do?"

"What he's always done, everything! I'll tell you what Ryan, if you're so worried, then you go work at the paper. Maybe he won't treat you like you're incompetent and seek out every mistake each morning."

Ryan opened his mouth to say more but Pippa quieted him with a hand on his thigh. "What will you do instead?"

"I'm working on a few things," I told her kindly, appreciative that she was being supportive. "I'll be fine. I won't do anything until my plan is fully fleshed out."

"I can't believe you're going to leave him high and dry."

"Screw you, Ryan. Would you stick around if the label suddenly wanted to record *only* other people's songs? Pop songs, sugary and repetitive?" We both knew the answer to that. "But it's all right for poor little Lacey, right?"

"I didn't say that."

"Yeah, you did actually. But thank you. It's nice to know that your opinion of me is no different than Daddy's. I'm out of here." I didn't stick around for his apologies or explanations, because I wouldn't believe them anyway. Instead of grabbing something delicious from Dark Horse, I left quickly and went straight home to contemplate my next move.

Now that I'd said the words out loud to Pippa and Ryan, they felt true. It was time to move on, to do my own thing, whatever that was. For starters, I spent the afternoon looking into blogging. There was more to it than just picking a quirky blog name and start typing, but I was confident it was something I could do, and hopefully earn some money doing it.

By the time Stevie came home from cheerleading practice, I had an outline of a plan, and I had a timeline to put it into action. Hopefully.

"Hey Stevie, how was your day?"

"Good!" She brightened up and started with her favorite part of the day, cheerleading practice. "I finally perfected my arabesque and went straight into a liberty stand. It was so cool, Mom."

"That's great, Stevie. I guess that summer camp was worth it."

Her smile widened. "Totally worth it. I learned so much, even Coach Matthews has noticed. What's for dinner?"

"Tacos. You can make the salsa." We worked in the kitchen with music playing in the background. Stevie and I were a team and we had been way before my marriage fell apart.

"The whole jalapeno or just half," she asked with a teasing smile.

"Seed half of it and use the whole thing. Unless you're too scared?"

Stevie jutted her chin out, looking a lot like her father. "Challenge, accepted."

I rolled my eyes. "It's your tummy, not mine."

"I said challenge accepted, didn't I?"

"We'll see, just don't come crying to me later." She stuck her tongue out at me.

"So," she wiggled her eyebrows and took the seat directly across from me before she started to build her first taco. "You and Levi, what's the deal?"

"No deal," I assured her. "We're colleagues, possibly

friends."

"Why? I like him. He's funny and charming and pretty decent looking for an old guy." She spoke like a dating expert and I couldn't help but laugh.

"You want me to date a decent looking old guy? Thanks kiddo."

"Mom," she whined and rolled her eyes. "It's okay if you want to date, I think you should. It's time."

It's only been six months, but everyone kept telling me that it was time to move on as if I was pining after my ex-husband. "It's been a few months."

"Mom it's been like two years. Don't wallow in this, please. It's not healthy."

"I'm not," I assured her. "I'm really not. It's not about your father, I'm just not sure that I'm ready to trust another person like that." Even though things with Martin had never been terrible, they had been bland and boring, but I'd trusted him not to hurt or betray me. And he had, terribly. "I'm happy though Stevie, so please don't waste a moment of your time worrying about me."

"You're my mom, of course I worry about you." She rolled her eyes as if that were the most obvious thing in the world. "But boys are fun. They can be funny, and they're cute. And Mr. Branson has lots of stories that will make you laugh, have a good time."

Levi was handsome and incredibly entertaining. But I shrugged off all thoughts of Levi. "We work together."

That was a bad idea, even if I had a plan in place to change that fact.

"All you do is work, Mom. Where else are you going to meet someone?"

"I go out and do stuff," I argued because I had a life. It wasn't exciting or anything, but I spent time with friends and that was very satisfying.

"Yeah, but Aunt Pippa and Aunt Valona are coupled up now."

A fact of which I was very well aware. But I narrowed my gaze at Stevie and wondered to myself where this was all coming from. "Are you trying to get me to lower your dating age, young lady?"

"Nope," she answered with a laugh. "But if you wanted to do that, I wouldn't object. Just so you know."

She was barely even a teenager and already a handful.

CHAPTER 8
LEVI

It was already past ten o'clock and Lacey still hadn't made an appearance at the office. Not that I was keeping track of her or anything, just that I'd turned my story in about the female lawyer and her troubles in town two days ago and I still hadn't heard a word from her.

About anything.

Dinner with Mickey and Stevie had gone well. So I figured it was the almost-kiss that had her hiding and avoiding me, which was really too bad because I'd been hoping for another chance at kissing her. Barring that, I hoped she didn't hate the story. It wasn't a typical story by Carson Creek Daily Journal standards, it was far more somber and much longer, but it was exactly my type of story.

"Hey GG, is everything all right with Lacey?" The old

man was too oblivious to realize he was losing his daughter, but he was my best shot at getting answers since he was the only other person in the office.

GG looked up as if he'd forgotten there was anyone else in the room and shrugged. "Nope. She doesn't tell me anything anymore."

Gee, I wonder why. The old man didn't do himself any favors where his daughter was concerned, but it wasn't my place to speak on it, and if Lacey found out she would probably have my head.

"All right." If GG hadn't heard anything then there wasn't anything to hear, and Lacey was fine, just avoiding me. Or GG.

Or both of us.

Twenty minutes later the clock struck quarter to eleven and Lacey strolled into the office almost as if on a breeze. She had on one of those shirt dresses that was both casual and sexy in the way it hugged her curves. The pale blue shade gave her eyes an added sparkle. Her legs were bare and she wore girlish canvas sneakers with blue polka dots. She entered the bullpen without her usual greeting, and not a glance was spared for me or GG. It was a version of Lacey that had never made an appearance at the office, and as much as I liked the way she looked, I had to bite back a sense of foreboding in my gut.

I gave her twenty minutes to settle in before I knocked on her door. "Come in, Levi."

I pushed open the door and smiled at the pretty picture she made, relaxed and smiling from behind her desk. "How did you know it was me?"

"GG always barges right in." She spoke the words simply, no anger or frustration, just a fact of her life.

"Right. Is everything okay Lacey?"

She nodded, her gaze suddenly focused on the computer screen. "Everything is fine. Why do you ask?"

"Just making sure everything was all right with you and Stevie. You're not normally late, and I was worried."

Her expression softened and Lacey waved me in. "I just had a few things I needed to take care of. Daddy can wait to tell me all the mistakes he found in today's paper." She motioned to the chair across from her. "Have a seat."

I kept my eyes on Lacey, which was no hardship, to see if her expression gave anything away, but she was a cool customer, calm and poised. Only the hint of strain around her pink lips told me something was weird. Off.

"You didn't give me any feedback on the story."

Lacey looked at me for a long time, her long lashes fanned dramatically when she blinked. "Oh. Right."

I braced myself, the way I always did, for her critique. "Okay, I'm ready."

Lacey's lips tugged into a small smile. "The story was wonderful, Levi. Wonderful and heartbreaking, and so maddening I wanted to rage on her behalf. Excellent work."

I was shocked and flattered by her words, the emotions my story had invoked in this woman. "Really?"

"Yes, really. In fact it's going to be a front page story, which I know you're used to, but hey, I guess I have to feed the ego too."

Her words teased a laugh out of me. "Mmm, ego hungry."

Her laughter mingled with mine but it faded just as quickly. "Your telling of her story brought tears to my eyes, Levi. This is a story the whole town will be talking about." She was serious and more importantly, her words were sincere.

"Thank you, Lacey. That means a lot coming from you." I still couldn't shake the idea that something was off, but I knew asking her outright wouldn't produce any answers. "I thought GG had a rule that only happy and upbeat stories go on the front page." He was determined to shy away from the *if it bleeds, it leads* mantra of most news organizations, but only happy news created the opposite problem.

She shrugged off my concern, but her brows dipped into a frown. "How is this not happy news? The women in this town and this county are finally getting a fair shot in court, and the proof of that is in how these abusive men are behaving."

She had a point, but Lacey was an intelligent woman and I knew her misunderstanding was on purpose.

"Okay," I said, slightly confused. "In that case, I'll take the compliment and the spot of honor."

"Ego satisfied?" The playful Lacey had returned and I felt my body relax into the chair.

"Not quite. The ego would love to celebrate over a delicious dinner with a beautiful companion."

Her cheeks turned an adorable shade of pink, but Lacey's blue gaze never wavered. "Your ego?"

"Me. I would like to have a celebratory dinner. With you."

"Why?"

"Because you're beautiful and funny, and I would like to get to know you better. And it's a ritual to celebrate every big thing, like a front-page story."

Lacey considered me carefully, and after about thirty seconds I knew she would shoot me down. She sighed in that way women do when they're trying to figure out how to let a man down easily and she shook her head.

"That would be great, actually. I know just the place for a foodie like you, and I think there's a salad or two on the menu."

Once her words finally sank in, I laughed. She was so fun and sassy, it was always great to be around her now that she'd warmed up to me. "I eat a lot more than salad, Lacey."

Her lips twitched in amusement, but she did a good job of keeping the laughter at bay. "I couldn't be sure of that, and I didn't want to offend you."

I laughed again and got up with a smile. "I'll pick you up at seven-thirty as long as I'm able to find a babysitter."

"I'll text Stevie to see if she'll do it, which I'm sure she will if you have some delicious world cuisine to offer her."

"I do. The good thing about cooking for one adult and one kid is that there's always leftovers."

Lacey smiled and I stood a little taller at the hint of appreciation in her eyes. "Then I'll see you at seven-thirty Levi."

I left the office feeling lighter and happier, but I couldn't stop my journalist's brain from churning, guessing all the reasons Lacey could be acting strangely.

None of them were good, but we had an entire evening together for me to figure it out.

CHAPTER 9
LACEY

The doorbell rang at exactly seven-thirty and I smiled to my reflection as I gave myself one final look before this *dinner not a date* officially got under way. I'd dressed carefully, probably too carefully, in a little red dress that showed off my curves, black lace cap sleeves that hid my less than toned arms. I finished the look off with four-inch black stilettos that gave me the legs of a twenty year old. Satisfied with what I saw, I turned to the door, took a deep breath and pulled it open.

The casual greeting died on my lips at the sight of Levi looking date-night hot. Gone was his standard checkered long sleeved shirt, jeans and comfortable brown shoes. Instead of his daily uniform, Levi had on dark gray slacks and a light green button up that highlighted the golden threads in his deep brown eyes.

"Levi, wow. You clean up well. Very well."

He flashed a satisfied smile, not bothering to hide the long appraising look that swept down my body and then back up. "You look gorgeous, Lacey. I'll be the luckiest guy at...where are we going again?"

I tried to ignore the heat his gaze ignited, but it was impossibly potent. "It's called a surprise, Levi. Just follow my directions and you'll be fine."

He laughed and took a step back as I stepped out to look the door. The heat of his look lingered on my backside like a living breathing thing between us.

"Bossy lady."

"Don't you forget it, mister."

"I won't," he promised and took my hand to help me into the passenger seat of his car. "Stevie and Mickey are all set with homemade chicken mole, rice and a bunch of other stuff. Mickey didn't even make a big deal out of a rerun dinner as he calls it."

I laughed as he told me all about Mickey's usual aversion to having leftovers for dinner. "So he doesn't mind eating them for lunch, but not dinner?"

"Exactly. Says he feels like he's missing out." Levi laughed again, that masculine sound intoxicating and contagious.

"Guess you men get picky earlier and earlier in life."

"I think I might be spoiling him. How is he going to enjoy a simple burger and fries or pizza after chicken mole?"

"Oh the horror, he won't have to deal with the health effects of a greasy, fast food diet. What a monster you are."

"Sarcasm," he said softly. "I like it."

The ride to the restaurant was good-natured and full of conversation, and I knew this dinner, whether it was a date or not, wouldn't be a disaster. Maybe Stevie and Pippa were right, it was time to get back on the proverbial horse.

Levi gasped, the sound more intrigued than surprised, and the heat in his brown eyes when he turned to me, produced an unconscious shiver. "What is this place?"

I flashed a satisfied smile and stepped from the car. "Let's go in and find out. I reviewed this place a few months ago and you're the only person I know, other than Stevie, who would appreciate it." The Japanese-Indian fusion restaurant was off the beaten path but usually, like tonight, it was packed with diners, loud with dozens of different conversations and plenty of laughter.

"Oh. My." Levi's surprise was even more genuine this time and I couldn't help but smile at having surprised him. "Japanese and Indian? This ought to be fun!"

It was exactly the response I hoped for and I looked forward to the evening ahead as we were lead to our table and ordered drinks. "I think we could both use some fun in our lives."

"Definitely that. Every day with Mickey is enjoyable, but grown up fun has been seriously lacking in my life."

"Same." I smiled and thought about his comment earlier in my office, that he wanted to get to know me better. I wanted the same. "So Levi, did you just fall into serious journalism or were those the stories that called to you?"

He blinked as if no one had ever asked that question before. "I guess a little of both. When I was younger and chasing prestige and recognition, I gravitated towards those stories, but once I started to tell those stories, I knew it was what I was meant to do. They deserve to have their stories told as much as anyone, maybe more than most. I'm proud of the effect my work had on their lives. Mostly."

"You're more impressive and less egotistical than I thought you'd be," I admitted sheepishly.

The smile he gifted me with was sexy and sincere, a mix I never thought would call to me or my libido. "Coming from you Lacey, that means a lot to me." He took a sip of turmeric Sake when it arrived and sighed. "What about you, Lacey, did you always want to be a journalist?"

I nodded. "Yes, but I had dreams of being more like you than GG. I wanted to write stories about people of the world, not just the serious stories, but also human interest pieces that were more different than an American audience could imagine. Things didn't turn out that way, though." Conversation paused while the server brought out a variety of small fusion dishes, from tandoori sushi to curry gyozas.

"Why not? I've read your stuff, and it's good. Well-written, insightful and full of life."

"Thanks." His words made me feel good as a woman and a professional. It's all I wanted, for the world to know that I was more than a little girl who'd gotten ahead because her daddy owned the paper. "I always thought, incorrectly of course, that GG would retire and I could change CCDJ a little bit, modernize the whole thing. I want to keep the small town feel of the paper, but add worldwide stories too." I sighed. "That sounds silly, doesn't it?"

"Not at all. You want the people of Carson Creek to feel safe at home but to know what's going on in the rest of the world? It's admirable."

"Yeah, I guess. At this point it's a non-starter. How are things going with Michelle?" It was a clumsy subject change, but thankfully Levi let it go.

"Mostly good. She's still not sure that I'm going to stick around, which is my fault, I know that. All I can do is show her by showing up. Otherwise, things are good."

"So you're happy with life in Carson Creek?"

He nodded, smiling around another bite of delicious food. "Very, and getting happier with it by the second."

Was Levi Branson flirting with me? It sure felt like it, but it had been so long, I couldn't really be sure. "Is that why you invited me to dinner, to get happy?"

Levi laughed again. "Get happy? That's a new euphemism for me, but sure, I wouldn't be opposed to getting happy with you Lacey. Of making you happy."

A shiver shot through me and I laughed. "Wow, that's pretty direct Levi."

"You think that's a good idea?" I wasn't exactly opposed to it either, but there were other factors to consider. "We work together."

"Things could get complicated."

"Possibly," I agreed, but in that moment with the way he looked at me, I wondered if complicated would be such a bad thing.

Conversation was put on pause as we debated having dessert, but the food was too good, too satisfying to stuff ourselves with sugar. "Maybe we can get something to go," he offered with a smile, his sing-song tone making even the server laugh.

I agreed with that plan, knowing Stevie and Mickey will be happy to test out the worldly desserts, and we paid the bill before exiting the restaurant. The night was warm even for early Spring, and the clear sky meant the stars shone as far as the eye could see.

"What a beautiful night." My heart raced with anticipation, of what I had no idea, at least not until Levi turned to me with an intense stare and longing in his eyes.

"Yes," he whispered and stepped in so close that his chest brushed against my aching nipples. "I'm going to kiss you now, Lacey." He gave me a heartbeat to react, which was more than enough time for me to know that I wanted to kiss this man, to pick up where we'd left off in my kitchen, only tonight I looked and felt beautiful. Tonight I was just a woman, letting a handsome man kiss her.

The kiss wasn't just a kiss thought, oh no, it was full of heat and longing. It was intense, and Levi's mouth devoured me hungrily, as if he'd been waiting an eternity for just this moment. Just this kiss. His lips were strong, firm but gentle, as they brushed against mine. His tongue was insistent and commanding, and I briefly wondered if that's what he would be like in bed.

That thought brought me up short. Was I seriously thinking about sleeping with Levi? A man who worked with me? A man who could get a new assignment and fly off to the far-flung wilds of Egypt on a moment's notice?

Hell yes.

The kiss was on the brink of being an all-consuming thing that threatened to spiral out of control, and we pulled back simultaneously, eyes wide, chests heaving with desire and the need for oxygen.

"That was...wow. Unexpectedly wow."

Levi chuckled. "It was," he sighed. "I wasn't sure you were interested."

"I was mildly interested, until now. But Levi we work together, so much could go wrong."

"Maybe it won't," he said with a casual shrug.

It would eventually, it always did in some way, shape or form. "I'm not opposed to seeing you again, kissing you again," I admitted. "But maybe we can keep this between us for a little while, at least until we know what it is?"

Levi's lips twisted into a playful, teasing grin. "Are you saying that you want to have a secret affair with me, Lacey Gregory?"

I laughed. "That's not exactly what I was getting at, but when you say it like that, it sounds pretty darn intriguing."

He brushed a hand down my hair and twirled a lock around his finger. "What were you getting at?"

"This is a small town Levi, and people have expectations that I'm not in the mood to deal with, but I'd like to see you again."

"And kiss me again?"

I nodded. "That too, maybe see if you do other things as well as you kiss, just not under a spotlight."

He leaned in and kissed me again, going deeper and deeper until a loud whistling sound followed by a smattering of applause startled us apart. "Then consider me on board with our secret affair."

Those words were just what I wanted to hear, and suddenly I felt bold and brazen, sensual. "There's a lookout spot on the way home where we can go and make out like teenagers."

"You want to seal the deal with a hot make out session? I should play the lottery tonight too, with all this luck."

Me too, because this handsome man falling into my lap has to be an act of karmic payback for not making my divorce as difficult as I could have, and according to some, should have.

Making out with Levi was more than worth that sacrifice.

CHAPTER 10
LEVI

"Levi Branson as I live and breathe!" A woman with very big, and very blond hair stopped at our table, interrupting time with my family. "I've been looking all over for you."

I didn't recognize her, which was strange in a town as small as Carson Creek, but still I smiled. "For what, exactly?"

Her light brown eyes sparkled. "So you can ask me out, of course." The woman was unashamed of her bold flirtations, which normally would have appealed to me in a temporary kind of way.

But now my thoughts were full of another blond, one with big blue, all-seeing eyes. I blinked in the face of her expectant expression. "I'm sorry, do I know you?"

"Not yet. I'm Paige, and I'm hoping a dinner can change all that."

Okay, then. I looked to my daughter Michelle and her barely contained laugh and back at Paige. "I'm sorry, now isn't a good time."

Paige's shoulders fell, but she recovered quickly. "Until we meet again, Levi." With a flirty finger wave, she sauntered off.

Finally, Michelle's laughter exploded and Mickey joined in even though he had no idea what was so funny. "Oh my god, she was so brazen!"

"What's brazen, Mama?" Mickey didn't want to be left out of even one moment of good times.

Michelle straightened, and after another few moments she was able to get herself under control enough to answer Mickey's question.

"It means she is bold, has courage and no shame."

Blond brows wrinkle in confusion. "What's shame?"

"I'll explain when you're older," she told her son and turned her attention to me, face twisted in curiosity. "That's the third woman to stop at our table and ask you out. You accepted none of their obvious invitations. Why?"

I shrugged at her question, because I wasn't ready to get into it now, if ever. "I'm just not interested. Is that so hard to believe?" My gaze left Michelle's and searched the pizza joint for something, anything else to focus on other than my daughter's studious gaze.

"Not hard to believe, but I'm curious...oh my god. You've already found someone." Her eyes were wide with a teasing mix of amusement and surprise. "Who is she? Is she from your travels? What's her name?"

I sighed, knowing the only way out of this interrogation was to give her a few details. "There is a woman, but it's new and she's not from my travels, she's a local." Lacey was more than a local, she was the epitome of Carson Creek living.

Michelle's expression shifted as the amusement faded and something like pride flashed in her eyes. "So you're not leaving for a while?"

I ignored the sting caused by her doubt, reminding myself that I'd earned that doubt the hard way. "Nope, not leaving. I'm here as long as you need me Michelle, I promise."

Her shoulders dropped in relief. "I'm sorry, Dad. It's just, I'm having a hard time believing it."

"It's all right. You have every right to doubt me, but I'm determined to make sure you never have a reason to doubt me again. Besides, Mickey's my best bud, what would I do without him?"

Mickey giggled. "I'm not going anywhere, Grandpa. I'm too little."

Michelle and I shared a laugh at his innocent words. "Neither am I kiddo." He giggled again and shook his head when I ruffled his hair.

"Hey Stevie!" Mickey spotted the girl first as she headed our way, bouncing with energy in her cheerleading uniform. "What're you doing here?"

She smiled at Mickey and gave him a wink. "Same as you. Pesto and cheese stuffed crust pizza."

Mickey gasped and looked to Michelle with wide, pleading eyes. "Mama?"

Stevie flashed an amused grin before turning to me. "Mr. Branson, I have to tell you again that the sushi was incredible. Really amazing. Anytime you want to teach me how to do it, I'm prepared to offer double babysitting duties."

"Okay," Mickey piped up and slid from the booth to wrap his arms around Stevie's waist. "When?"

Stevie looked down at Mickey with an affectionate smile. "Soon I'm guessing, which is good, because I found a book I used to love when I was your age and I think you'll love it too."

Satisfied with Stevie's answer, Mickey climbed back into the booth and went back to coloring on the table mat.

Stevie grinned at Michelle. "You must be his Mama?"

Michelle laughed at the girl's boldness, and nodded. "Am I famous?"

"Kid famous for sure. He talks about you all the time. What kind of doctor are you studying to be?"

"Probably general surgery, but I'm still in the figuring it out stage of medical school."

Stevie nodded thoughtfully. "How hard is it, really?"

"Very hard, especially if you're not studying medicine for the right reasons, but when you get where I am now, you know most of what you need to do the job."

"Super cool." Stevie flashed a smile, a look of awe in her eyes. "You must be crazy smart."

Michelle blushed. "Or just plain crazy."

Stevie joined in. "My mom says if you don't think what you're doing is a little bit crazy, it's probably not worth doing."

I wonder if that applied to our recently agreed upon affair.

"Let's go Stevie!"

She looked over her shoulder and back to the table with a smile. "Gotta go stretch and practice before the game this afternoon. Hope to see you guys there. Catch ya later, Mickey."

"Bye Stevie!"

With one final wave, she bounced off to meet with her cheerleader friends and exited the restaurant in a wave of giggles and whispers.

During the lull in conversation, which I knew was temporary while Michelle figured out her next approach, our food arrived. Pizza for the table and an order of curly fries for me. "Thanks. Refills all around please." The server nodded and walked off with a smile.

"So Dad, you have some news you want to share?"

"No," I growled around a piping hot bite of cheese and sausage pizza.

"We made gizas for Miss Lacey and Stevie, and Grandpa left sushi for me and Stevie."

I sent my grandson a playful glare. "Thanks, kid."

"You're welcome, Grandpa." The boy chewed his pizza happily, unaware he'd just given away all of my secrets.

"Really?" Michelle turned to me with a teasing grin. "Miss Lacey, as in your boss, Lacey Gregory?"

"One and the same," I confirmed and took another bite of pizza, a bigger bite than necessary to give myself time to think, and an excuse to not to have to offer up any more details.

"Interesting," was all she said as she carefully finished off her first slice.

"It doesn't mean I'm not committed to helping take care of Mickey. He is my priority."

"Oh I know that," she replied, expression suddenly serious. "I'm not worried."

"You're not?"

"Nope. I'm actually impressed, Dad. Lacey is beautiful and smart, and she's really sweet."

I frowned. "You know her?"

"Not much, but she did a small story when I started medical school, asking anyone in town who could help me to do it, and the town rallied."

I smiled at the thought of Lacey, champion of women, committing such an act of kindness for my kid. "She never said."

"That doesn't seem like her style. She wouldn't even accept my thanks, said it was her pleasure to do all she could to help a future doctor achieve her goals." Michelle laughed again. "You might be in over your head, Dad."

Don't I know it. "Stop hoarding my curly fries," was my only response.

Michelle laughed again, but she gracefully accepted the change in conversation.

CHAPTER 11
LACEY

What am I actually doing?

This question tap danced through my mind at least a dozen times as I drove away from the Daily Journal offices towards my house, knowing that Levi would be just a few minutes behind me. My nerves were completely frazzled at the thought of what would likely happen this afternoon, probably right after the lunch Levi promised he would bring with him.

This is crazy.

It was completely and totally crazy, but as I rushed inside and up the stairs, I felt thrilled at the possibility of having sex for the first time in years. Years. "Crap." I stared at the sexy lingerie I'd pulled from the back of my drawer, tags still on because I never got the chance to wear it before everything fell apart. The red lace stared back at me, almost mockingly, but I yanked the tags off and slipped it on before dressing again in the same t-shirt dress I'd worn to the office.

I smiled, suddenly I felt sexy, so much so that I walked with a bit more confidence as I made my way back downstairs to wait for Levi. The lace was soft against my sensitized skin and my breath hitched as it scraped over my suddenly hard nipples.

The doorbell rang and goosebumps popped out all over my skin. *Breathe in, breathe out.* My legs shook a little as I walked to the door and opened it, trying to appear as cool and relaxed as I could.

"Levi. You took your time getting here, didn't you?"

He laughed, his gaze raked over my body several times before he responded. "I figured we could both use a little bit of anticipation."

Damn, he's good. "I think we've been anticipating this for days already."

Levi laughed and stepped inside, forcing me to step back. "You smell good. Damn good."

What in the hell was wrong with me? Every move, every look, every moment with this man created awareness that hit each part of my body with a shot of lust. "Th-thank you." I swallowed hard and risked a look up at Levi, his brown eyes filled with heat and desire.

He closed the door and motioned for me to lead the way, allowing me to direct where this afternoon was headed. "Is this weird for you?"

"A little, I think. I'm not sure I'm thinking all that clearly at the moment though."

Levi set the bag down and turned with a questioning look. "You're having second thoughts?"

"No, I'm more than a little...turned on."

His smile came slow and hot, like the first stages of an inferno. "Let's see if we can remedy that a little." Without warning, his hands rested on my shoulder and slid up my neck until his big hands cupped my face, holding me like I was something precious. And a moment later, his mouth was on mine, devouring my lips right along with my good sense.

I sank into his kiss, pressed against his big body in search of any kind of relief from the storm gathering within me. I moaned when his tongue swept inside my mouth and I quivered as his hands began to roam my curves with the kind of appreciation that made a woman feel truly desired.

I want this.

The thought invaded my mind and it was the only thing I could think about, other than how good it felt to be held and kissed by a man again. So good. Almost too good. I pulled back with a needy groan. "Levi."

"Too much?" His lips curled into a satisfied smile as if he knew the words I would say next.

"It's great, but I'm sorry to say Levi that it is not...enough."

His smile broadened and his eyes darkened to black

orbs of desire as he dove in for another kiss, this time his hands kicked up their exploration. His big, warm fingers slid down my back until his hands cupped my considerable backside, adding a growl of appreciation to the mix before they slid up to my waist, holding me like I was a tiny little thing, which was how I felt against Levi's size. Finally his hands roamed up and around to cup my breasts, heavy with desire, before his thumbs grazed my nipples.

"This body," he growled. "It's perfection. I need to see it."

I smiled, feeling bolder than I'd ever felt in my life as I took two steps back and grabbed the hem of my dress. "Need?"

Levi nodded like a man possessed. "You have five seconds before I do it myself."

His words sent a shiver through me, and I didn't even bother to hide it as I slowly pulled the dress up and over my head. My heart raced when the dress was off and I stood under the dark, hot perusal of Levi's eyes over my body.

"Well?"

"Red is definitely your color." He closed the gap between us and slid his tongue along the seam of the bra where cleavage met fabric. His tongue was magical as it worked from one breast to the other before licking down my stomach where he pressed a kiss to the triangle between my thighs. "Definitely your color."

"Levi," I moaned.

"Say my name like that every time you say it. Please."

I looked at him. "Kiss me like that every time, and I will."

My words were rewarded with an open-mouthed kiss right over my panties which provided delicious friction.

"Good god, Levi."

His low chuckle sent vibrations ricocheting through me and my fingers tangled in his hair, gripping perhaps a little too hard. With another laugh, his lips dotted heat up my body until his mouth was on mine again.

"Lacey."

"Levi." His name came out as a breathless whisper, our lips still touched. "Naked. Now. Please."

He took a step back, slowly undressing until he stood before me in nothing but a pair royal blue boxer briefs. His body was...incredible. Long and lean, almost rangy with his long muscles and tanned skin. But it was the dark hair on his chest and the long trail that disappeared behind his boxer briefs that reminded me that Levi was a man.

All man.

"Wow. This is unexpected." My gaze roamed his body to the point I was ogling him, I couldn't look away from the long ridge of arousal pushing against the fabric of his underwear.

"Keep looking at me like that and this will be over before it even begins."

My hand reached out to touch his chest and I dragged my fingertips down his abs before gripping the erection doing a bad job of hiding behind his boxers.

"Lacey," he growled and hooked a hand around my waist to pull me flush against him.

"Yes, Levi?" I continued to stroke him through his underwear, but it wasn't enough. I needed more.

He bent and gripped my thighs, lifting me up and carrying me to the sofa with a growl. "Bedroom. Where is it?"

"Upstairs, last door on the left." I was breathless as Levi carried me up, a dark look on his face as he laid me on the bed and stared down at me, hungry and aroused. "Come here." I channeled my inner vixen and summoned him.

His body laid over mine, the delicious weight a good reminder of all that I'd missed in the past few years. He was hard everywhere I was soft, and I shook as his lips kissed me all over before he slid one finger deep enough to send my back arching off the bed. "All that delicious wetness, just for me."

I covered my face at his naughty words. "Levi!"

"Too much?" He looked down at me, finger still thrusting in and out of me slowly. Deeply.

I panted and shook my head. "No, it's good. Really, really good." My hips rolled on their own and Levi added another long finger. "Goodness!" My hips bucked up and his fingers slid deeper still. "Wow."

Levi flashed a devilish smile at my reaction, his smile darkened when I reached down to shove his boxers down his hips. "You sure?"

"Very sure." I was nervous but excited, and as Levi's body covered mine once again, his hips spreading my own, I felt myself tense in anticipation. "Don't tease," I whined.

He sent me a crooked smile and licked his lips as his hips moved in shallow thrusts against my opening and sometimes my clit. "Who's teasing?" He did it over and over again until I was gasping and breathless.

"Levi," I groaned and that was the moment he chose to slide in deep, so achingly slow and so deep I shuddered. He filled me up, deliciously so. He was long and thick and his strokes so efficient that I felt my orgasm rising quickly.

His jaws tightened and his gaze darkened. "You're so tight."

His words weren't even dirty, but they ramped up my arousal and I felt even more of him as I tightened and pulsed around him. "My goodness."

His lips tightened into a satisfied, purely masculine smile as his hips began to move faster and faster, his strokes going deeper to hit that one special spot that made me temporarily blind.

"Let go, Lacey. I've got you."

I let myself trust him in that moment, and when he leaned over to taste my nipples, I did what he said. I let go. My first orgasm in more than two years seemed to go on for two years, my body shook and vibrated, all while Levi continued to pound into me. "Levi." His name came out on a strangled moan that tugged another lopsided smile on his lips.

Levi was a picture of masculine beauty above me, jaws clenched, eyes focused on me while his body thrust in and out in search of the same pleasure that swamped me. He was so gorgeous with his face twisted in agony and I gave myself permission to touch him, to taste him as he sent my body up another mountain where my second orgasm was just out of reach.

My teeth sank into his shoulder and Levi's control finally snapped, he lifted my leg over his hip and thrust so deep my eyes fluttered shut and pleasure took over. Faster and faster he moved and when I came the second time, he grunted in pleasure soon after.

"Lacey," he collapsed on top of me. "Holy shit."

I smiled. "Yeah?" It was good for me, I knew that, but was it really that good for him. "Really?"

He nodded against my shoulder. "Hell yeah. I think I might have to check my heart after this."

I smiled. "I wasn't sure. It's been a long time for me."

"I felt it," he whispered in my ear and I shivered. "You were so tight I had to think about war to keep from coming too soon."

I laughed. "Stop."

"Can't," he groaned as he slowly pulled out and dropped to his side, pulling me with him. "I'll have dreams about sliding into you for weeks. Possibly months."

I rolled my eyes, but I felt myself blush.

"How long?"

I could have pretended I didn't know what he was talking about, but this wasn't the time for dishonesty. "Two years and some months."

"Impossible! You're gorgeous, are the men in this town blind and stupid?"

His outrage justified my own similar feelings. "No. Women my age aren't exactly a hot commodity, you know."

Levi laughed and let his fingertips brush the side of my body from mid-thigh up to the side of my breast. "From where I'm sitting you're the hottest commodity in town."

"Flatterer."

"Honest," he shot back. "You're beautiful and smart, and sometimes you're funny."

"Hey, *sometimes*?"

He laughed. "Maybe you don't give out vibes that say you're interested."

"You weren't scared away," I insisted.

"I spent the last three decades of my life dodging bombs and bullets, being surrounded by poverty and hunger, I can handle a beautiful surly woman. And rejection."

"I'm so glad you did."

"Me too," he growled and pulled me closer until I was flat on my back, his naked body covered mine, his erection nudging my entrance. "So damn glad." After another round of pleasure, we made our way downstairs to eat the forgotten lunch still sitting on my coffee table.

"I hope you got a lot of food, because I have certainly worked up an appetite."

Levi laughed. "I planned ahead."

I smirked and arched a brow at him. "So confident in your skills?"

He shrugged. "I was thinking more like fuel for the event, and then refueling to return to work."

"I like the way you think Levi Branson."

"Do you like what I'm thinking right now?" He wiggled his eyebrows and I laughed again.

"I don't know, why don't you show me?"

He did just that, and then we returned to work. An hour late.

CHAPTER 12
LEVI

Was twenty-four hours too soon to request another afternoon with Lacey? I didn't know the rules to our secret relationship, or if there were any rules beyond keeping it secret. I just knew that I wanted to see her again. Hell, after yesterday I was pretty sure that no amount of time would be enough time with her. The woman had done more than turn my head, she'd flipped me on my back with her sensuality, her zest for pleasure—giving and receiving—and her playful nature.

I was a goner.

I'd spent most of yesterday afternoon trying not to stare at her as she walked through the newspaper offices, forcing myself to picture her in the dress she was wearing, instead of the sexy red lingerie I knew was underneath it. It was a Herculean task only made manageable by the fact that her cantankerous father was also seated in the bullpen, ever present scowl on his face. That, and I had to leave to pick up my grandson.

Today was a new day, and the first thing on my mind after getting Mickey off to daycare was how to get Lacey alone again for a few hours. I made it into the office later than usual because I had a meeting at Old Country House with Carlotta to discuss a write-up on the venue's website about the ease of all-in-one venues, and foregoing the traditional travel between church and reception hall weddings. It was just past eleven when I started up the steps to the office, but halfway up I heard shouting. Very loud shouting.

I hurried up the steps to find Lacey and GG arguing so fiercely I was sure one of them would end up dead. I was ready to break up the fight, but they were in Lacey's office, door open just enough to hear everything.

"You can *not* run a story like this on the first page Lacey! What in the hell were you thinking?"

"I was thinking that this is a beautifully written story that deserves to be told with maximum exposure, since we don't have an online edition, the front page was the best and *only* option."

"That's no excuse little girl!"

I cringed at his condescending tone and braced myself for hurricane Lacey, only there was silence.

"It is a perfectly valid *reason* to publish the story, and

since you can't be bothered to actually run this paper, I made a judgment call."

"Your judgment is off, if that's the case." GG snorted derisively and I could picture Lacey rolling her eyes.

"You know what Daddy? If you don't like the choices I make about the Daily Journal, feel free to do all of this yourself since you clearly don't trust me to do any damn thing!"

"Hey, you watch your tone when you talk me girl, I'm still your Daddy."

"No, right now you are a stubborn old man who has an allergic reaction to change." I can picture her shaking her head in disgust, and then I heard it, the sound of her palms as they smacked against her desk. "I feel like a glorified layout specialist."

More silence before GG grunted out a response. "What's wrong with you lately? You didn't used to have a problem doing things the right way."

"Your way," she clarified. "You mean *your* way, not the right way. And you know what, GG? It doesn't matter what's wrong with me. You want what you want, and that's what I'm giving you. This is a good story, which is why you hired Levi isn't it?"

"We don't do these kinds of stories Lacey." GG's voice and his tone were tired, almost defeated. "You know that. Don't you?"

There was a lull in the argument, and though I

wasn't crazy enough to think it was over, I felt the need to intervene. "Is everything all right in here?"

Lacey's expression softened when she saw me in the doorway but only for a fraction of a moment. "Everything is fine, Levi. GG here was just telling me that this isn't a newspaper, but a human interest magazine. We don't report on anything serious, just the goings on in town like the Spring Fling dance and which charity groups reached their fundraising goals. So you see, no problem at all." She was angry, no it was more like furious.

"That is not what I said and you know it! Don't put words in my mouth girl."

"Maybe you just don't like how your words sound when it's not your lips saying them. Are we done here?" She stared down her father like a warrior, and she was beautiful with fire shooting from her eyes. "I mean you've already told me how much I screwed up, again, and since we don't have an online version to correct, this is all just an exercise to let you puff your chest out. So, are we done?"

GG snorted his disbelief and shook his head. "I don't know what's gotten into you lately Lacey, but you better fix that attitude and fast." With a shake of his head, GG left the office still griping under his breath.

"Sorry you had to hear all that, but it couldn't be helped."

I shrugged. "I've heard worse. You gonna be okay?"

"Me?" She nodded, her smile falsely bright and as phony as a two dollar bill. "I'm just peachy Levi. Just peachy."

"Hmmm," was all I said in response.

Her expression shifted to playful. "So, Levi are you here for business or pleasure?"

I stood a little taller. "Didn't realize pleasure was on the table so...both?"

"Good answer. Close the door. We have to be quick about it, GG doesn't stray too far from the offices these days."

My smile beamed bright as I closed her office door, and locked it. "What the lady wants...," I began and stalked towards her.

"Oh, the lady wants. She wants a lot."

I laughed and set about giving Lacey what we both wanted.

CHAPTER 13
LACEY

"Things must be really bad if you invited me to lunch." Carlotta flashed a bright, beauty queen smile as she slid into the booth seat beside Valona. I'd arrived at the diner early to get the most private spot I could find just before the late afternoon lunch rush hit.

I shrugged at her playful words. "I need multiple points of view." The truth was that I didn't need any points of view, not really. After the fight with Daddy yesterday, I was pretty dead set on my course. "First, how are you ladies doing?"

Valona smiled the smile of a well-loved and thoroughly satisfied woman still in the honeymoon stage of her relationship. "I'm good. Exhausted, but business is picking up, which is in part because Trey can't seem to turn down any business. The girls are growing too quickly and I feel like I don't spend enough time with my friends."

"Oh no," Carlotta rolled her eyes. "I'm getting so much hot sex and money that I can't find time for my oldest and dearest. We should all have your problems, Val."

"Hey," Valona frowned and shoulder bumped Carlotta.

"Come on honey, you're know we're all happy for you, and sure maybe a teensy weensy bit jealous."

"You have no reason to be jealous, Carlotta. You're amazing at a job you love, you always look fabulous and everyone loves you."

"Everyone except one special someone," she added with a wistful smile. "He hasn't landed in my lap yet, so I'm happy with my place in the world, for now. But you sugar, you are living the dream." Carlotta turned to me with a gleam in her eye. "And you, Lacey, have been holding out."

I blinked. "What are you talking about?"

"Hmmm," was all she said, but her assessing gaze bored a hole right through me. "Levi."

"What about him?"

"Nothing except that I personally witnessed three different eligible bachelorettes give him some of their best moves, which he was completely impervious to."

Why that thought gave me such relief, I wasn't ready to explore. Yet. "Maybe they weren't his type, Carlotta."

"Maybe," she conceded. "I even thought of that myself so I decided to do a little experiment. I flirted. Batted my eyelashes and poked my chest out, all the classics. I even went for straightforward no strings sex, and instead of being even a little bit intrigued, he looked uncomfortable, and worse, uninterested." Carlotta sat back with a smug smile. "So, spill."

Valona stared at Carlotta and blinked. "You're interested in Levi?"

"Heavens, no. I mean he's handsome in that rugged, spends-most-of-his-time-outdoors sort of way, but I like my men a bit more refined or a lot less refined if you get my drift."

I burst out laughing, and that drew a few stares, mostly from smiling old-timers who used the diner as their hub to catch up on gossip and gather more for later. "You don't have to say that when your drift is so overt, Carlotta."

"Enough deflecting, what's going on with you and the handsome journalist?"

"Nothing." Immediately I realized my mistake. I answered too quickly and with too much certainty, which wasn't my style, and now even Valona stared at me with suspicion.

"She'll tell us when she's ready. For now I'll settle for knowing what's got you all twisted up?"

"I don't know," I lied. "I'm just curious how you both decided to buck tradition. Carlotta you come from a family of lawyers, how did you go against the grain to become a party planner?"

She shrugged. "Truthfully? My family never expected much from me as long as I was pretty, polite and well-mannered, all the things a proper southern gentleman wants in a wife. The fact that I wanted a career at all was a surprise to them, so imagine their surprise to learn I'm good at my job. It took them a long time, too long, to acknowledge I was a success in my own right, and now Mama flies me out to Mississippi every December to plan her charity gala."

Hoping for that level of acceptance from GG was about as realistic as asking for the moon, which meant acceptance was off the table. "And you, Val?"

She shrugged. "Necessity mostly. I didn't need the money, but I needed a purpose, a reason besides the girls to get up each day. I always wanted to be a photographer, and without anyone telling me it was a ridiculous and unrealistic way to earn a living, I decided to go for it."

I was already in my chosen field, just not in the capacity I wanted, and if nothing changed, which it wouldn't as long GG had a say, then I had to force the change myself. I had to do this or else I would spend my life regretting every significant choice I'd ever made.

"I'm thinking of leaving the paper."

"Because of Levi?" Carlotta's long lashes fanned in her blinking disbelief.

"No, because of Daddy. I thought I would be running the paper by now, bringing it into the twenty-first century, but I'm starting to realize that's never going to happen."

"Have you spoken to him?" Val's eyes were wide with concern behind her glasses?

I nodded. "More than once. We got into a huge fight yesterday over Levi's front page story."

"On Adrienne Sands? That was such a wonderful yet tragic story," Carlotta exhaled, hand to her chest like an overwhelmed southern gentlewoman.

"It was fantastic," Valona agreed. "I was surprised to see it in the Daily Journal, to be honest."

"Exactly! That was why we fought, that story isn't the kind we usually print, and definitely not on the front page. The problem is that I've been waiting twenty years to do stories just like that. We're just not on the same page. Period." I tried not to revisit the anger I felt yesterday when he repeatedly called me a little girl, because it only highlighted my greatest fear, that he would never see me as capable of running the paper without him.

"Sounds like your mind is already made up." Carlotta's words were more certain than I felt.

"I know that I have to do it, and I've got things lined up to make the jump, but it's not that easy." I'd worked beside Daddy since high school, helping run the paper and secure ads. He'd even let me run the police blotter my senior year in high school. "It feels disloyal to leave."

Valona reached out and put her soft hand on top of mine. "But it sounds like staying would be a level of hell for you."

"Good for you," Carlotta added. "Don't stay to please GG if he doesn't appreciate your presence. You'll never get what you want from him, so you have to find a way to change your relationship to one you won't regret when he's gone."

Carlotta's words stuck with me for a long time after lunch was over, and the more I sat with them, the happier I was that I'd already purchased a domain name, consulted a web designer and looked into ways to monetize the site beyond subscriptions.

Things were coming together nicely, which made me feel better about looking out for my future. I didn't want GG to ever die, obviously, but I also didn't want death to be the way I finally got to run the paper the way I wanted. So my choice was simple, it was time to leave the only job I'd ever had.

Since I'd avoided the office—and GG—for most of the day, I decided to go home and jot down a few ideas on stories I wanted to write for my new venture. I had plenty of ideas over the years, and many of them came back to me as soon as I started the list, but after a while the ideas fizzled out completely.

"Dammit." Why was it easier to come up with

human interest stories for the Daily Journal every single day than to come up with a few interesting stories? "Because Daddy broke me." Was I even capable of writing hard-hitting stories anymore? "Dammit!"

I glanced at the clock and my shoulders sank in relief. Stevie had cheerleading practice for another hour, and then a study session, which gave me two hours to pick the brain of the best journalist I knew.

"Lacey." Levi's surprised but welcoming smile told me that coming to him was the right decision. "This is a treat."

He was a treat for the eyes in his gray V-neck sweater that almost made him seem like the stuffy professor type if not for the checkered collared shirt he wore underneath. His legs were hugged snugly by a pair of much beloved jeans, feet in nothing but a pair of cotton socks. "Are you busy?"

"For you I always have time." His smile was pure seduction and I couldn't help but blush even as I rolled my eyes.

His smile gave away what was on his mind, and even though sex wasn't why I was on his doorstep, seeing him now, it wasn't off the table. "Intimate time?"

Levi shrugged and took a step back, motioning for me to enter. "I won't say no, but it looks like you have something else on your mind."

An intuitive man that could shelve sex in favor of

conversation? I needed to keep my head on straight because this man was dangerous. "I do."

"Mickey conked out on the sofa, so let me get him put to bed upstairs and then I'm all yours."

All yours.

Why that sounded so appealing was another topic to be shoved away until a later date.

A much later date.

CHAPTER 14
LEVI

Something was on Lacey's mind, and I was sure that whatever it was had to do with the reason she'd been a ghost in the office today. She hadn't shown up and hadn't called, only sent me an email with the publishing needs for tomorrow's edition. Yet she'd come to see me, to talk.

I left her downstairs to gather her thoughts while I removed Mickey's clothes and traded them in for pajamas. He was so sweet and quiet when he was sleeping, but not nearly as fun as when he was awake.

This is my life now, I thought with a smile, and the truth was that I didn't regret it at all. The traveling was the only thing I missed, but now I could travel for fun, maybe find beauty and enjoyment in parts of the world where I'd only found chaos and destruction previously.

Mickey was a great kid, not to mention a reminder of what I'd missed while Michelle grew up.

At the top of the stairs I listened for signs of Lacey browsing photos of Michelle and Mickey, or giving herself a tour and heard nothing but silence. She was stuck in her head, and I gave myself a few moments of deep breathing before I went to hear whatever it was she needed to talk about.

"Hey, is everything all right?"

She stood at the fireplace staring with unseeing eyes for a long moment before she turned to me with a too bright smile that didn't quite meet her baby blue eyes.

"Hey yourself. How was your day?"

I shrugged casually at her question. If Lacey needed some small talk to get her started, I could do that. "Boring without something pretty to look at. GG was grumpier than usual, which gave me time to work up a few story ideas. How was your day?"

She sent me a playful, lopsided smile. "Boring without something pretty to look at, but otherwise productive."

"That sounds good. And ominous." I dropped down on the sofa and patted the seat beside me, but Lacey took the seat at the end of the sofa and tucked one foot underneath her, blue eyes glued to my face.

"What was your first story, and how did you choose it?"

"I didn't choose it, it was assigned to me. It was about the bodies that lined a street down in Mexico, suspected cartel murders." It was a crazy time, those cowboy days when thousands of journalists from around the world worked hard days and long hours to get their story told first. "It wasn't what it seemed, at least not to me."

"I remember it. You figured out that the majority of the victims had no relation to the cartels or associates. You theorized it was a serial killer. How?"

"By talking to the families of some of the victims. Many were too poor to have any real association with the cartel who pays for work and loyalty. Someone living the way many of those families did would have no reason to be loyal to them." I shook my head thinking of the poverty many of them lived in. "And the ones that couldn't be associated to a cartel were too similar to be anything else."

She nodded soaking up every word as if they were gospel. "And how did you choose the slant of that article, or any article really?"

I knew what she was asking, but she hadn't quite phrased it to indicate she knew what she was asking. "I don't have a slant to the story until after I've gathered all the facts."

She smiled softly. "You wrote Adrienne's story about the women who didn't get the justice they deserved until Adrienne became another victim of the men who'd been victorious in court, on both sides. It was a brilliant way to write the story, and not at all the story I expected you to tell."

I smiled, flattered at the compliment. "You gave me the bones of the story, but only after speaking with Adrienne at length and hearing her side of it, her perspective about losing in court, did the story reveal itself." It was an article I was proud to put my name on, and brought home the realization that I could do the same work without traveling the world. "What's with all the questions Lacey?"

Her eyes met mine, steady and clear. "I can't stay at CCDJ, not for much longer anyway. It's killing me, slowly every single day, so I'm dabbling with the idea of doing something similar for myself."

My heart sank at her words even though I was proud of her for leaving something that wasn't working for her. "You're going to another paper? In another town?" Whatever was happening between us had only just gotten started, and I wasn't ready to say goodbye.

"No, I can't. Stevie's whole life is here, and I don't want to uproot her." She nibbled her bottom lip, a surefire sign of anxiety. And guilt. "Maybe I'm also scared to leave, I don't know Levi, all I know for sure is that I can't spend many more days working for Daddy. You heard how many times he called me *girl* or *little girl* yesterday?"

I nodded. "It was hard not to hear that." It was also demeaning as hell, and meant to put her in her place. "I support your decision Lacey. If that's what you think is right for you, I support you."

She smiled and her whole demeanor softened at my words. "Yeah?"

I nodded. "Hell yeah. You have to do what's right for you, and unlike me, you're finding a way to do it without leaving your kid behind."

"You're too hard on yourself, Levi. It was a bad choice, but you made it and got an enviable career out of it. You can't go back and change it, but what you're doing is just as good."

"Right," I snorted.

"It's true. Without your help Michelle might have to drop out when she's so close to the finish line."

"She told me that you turned her into a local celebrity and encouraged the whole town to help however they could."

Lacey laughed and shook her head. "She was up to her eyeballs in casseroles. But Michelle is your daughter, which means she's stubborn and felt as if she was taking advantage of people after a while."

"Me? Stubborn? How dare you!"

She laughed as I meant her to and slid halfway across the sofa until our bodies touched from shoulder to knee. "Yeah, you. What you're doing now is giving her a chance at a life without unnecessary struggle. Now that you're here she can be the best doctor she can be."

I wrapped an arm around her, smiling to myself

when Lacey leaned her head on my shoulder, her sweet floral scent worked its way into my memory. I thought she might cry, but Lacey was a tough woman, and not just because she'd grown up with three rowdy brothers. "You have to do what's right for you Lacey, not GG or anyone else, but you and Stevie."

"You don't think I'm a disloyal daughter?"

I laughed. "Hell no. I've bounced around to so many publications because I don't believe in being loyal to people who don't return the favor. If GG wanted you to stick around, his behavior would reflect that, but it seems to me he's more interested in having you just execute his orders."

"Yeah," she sighed. "That's how I feel too."

"It's a shitty way to feel, worse when your own family is the reason."

"Ain't that the truth?" She sighed again and looked up at me. "I feel bad about leaving because I've always been the good daughter, the one that did her duty, but where has it gotten me?"

"You got what you needed from the experience, enough to know it's not how you want to spend the rest of your career."

Lacey looked up at me with an expression full of awe and affection, and surprisingly, I didn't mind. "You have a unique way of looking at things, Levi."

"Not so unique," I assured her. "I look at you and I

see a strong and capable, beautiful woman who can do just about anything she sets her mind to."

"Thank you, Levi."

"My pleasure," I sighed and pressed a kiss to her forehead, because I was honored to be the one she came to when she needed someone, hell I was flattered that I was that person for anyone.

"Want to make out?"

I pulled her closer until our lips were separated by less than a breath. "I thought you'd never ask."

She giggled and pressed her lips to mine and wrapped her arms around me tightly, kissing me as if this was more than a secret affair, more than scratching an itch.

And once again, I didn't mind.

Not even a little bit.

CHAPTER 15

LACEY

"Hey Mom?" Every mother in the world knew that tone. It was the sound of a child preparing to ask a favor. A big favor.

"Yes, Stephanie?" And every mother on the planet used their child's name, their full name, using the same tone.

"Don't full name me, Mom. Please." For good measure, Stevie rolled her eyes. "I just want to ask if I can spend the night at Sarah's on Friday night. Her mom already said it was all right because we have to leave *so early* to make it to the competition on time." Stevie paused for a moment, expecting me to give her all the reasons why she couldn't have a sleepover with one of her closest friends. "Staying over on Friday night is better for everyone, including you Mom." The smirk she sent my way was identical to her father's and for the first time, that didn't bother me.

"Sure. You and I will have dinner together on Friday, and then I'll take you to Sarah's. Deal?"

She looked up with a wide beaming smile. "Thanks Mom, you're the best."

"I really am, aren't I?"

"Mom," she groaned and rolled her eyes again. "Please."

"Oh I see, now that you've gotten your way the compliments go away." I let out a long suffering sigh, barely able to contain my laughter.

Stevie played her part beautifully and ignored my histrionics. "What's for dinner?"

"I was thinking peanut butter and jelly. Grape or strawberry."

"Gross."

I barked out a laugh and shook my head. "Give a girl a little bit of homemade sushi and suddenly she's Alton Brown."

"I don't know who that is, but what's wrong with wanting something delicious and different for dinner?"

"Nothing. In fact, you should consider learning to prepare a meal or two. It's a very grownup thing to do." There was no way I would pay premium prices for ingredients I didn't use often. "Nothing exotic tonight, just roasted chicken and vegetables with homemade biscuits."

Stevie looked up from her phone in shock. "*You* made biscuits. You?"

"Is that so hard to believe?"

"No," she admitted with a reluctant sigh. "But you never cook like this."

"That's because you don't appreciate it as far as I can tell, staring at your screen while you eat." It was like walking a tightrope, finding a way to encourage a young woman to eat healthy without feeding into her built-in insecurities. On most days it was an impossible task.

"I totally appreciate it, especially tonight. Tomorrow is Friday and I need to carb up so I'll have tons of energy to deal with a building full of cheerleaders for two days straight."

"You are one of those cheerleaders," I reminded her with a laugh.

"Yes," she sat up a little taller just as the oven timer sounded. "But I'm not perky all of the time."

"I know that better than anyone."

"Mom," she rolled her eyes again and I was tempted to bust out the old *your eyes will get stuck that way* joke, which I knew would go unappreciated.

I just laughed at her overall put upon demeanor and pulled dinner from the oven. "Tell me about school while you grab silverware and drinks."

"School is school," she insisted and pushed away from the table. "My grades are good, which you already know, and I'm thinking about joining student government. Do you think I can do it?"

"Stevie, you are bubbly and beautiful, kind and smart, you absolutely have what it takes to win. But do you have any ideas to make you good at the job?"

"I have a few ideas like allowing students to study during lunch. Not everyone has a quiet home, or you know, like a home where they can properly study so it's unfair to them."

"That is an excellent idea, honey. It's nice that you're thinking of the students that don't have what you do."

She shrugged off the compliment, but the blush on her cheeks told me she'd gotten the message. "I learned from the best," she sighed and her lips twisted into her famous worried look.

"What's wrong?"

"Nothing. I mean, it's just that I was hoping to skip dad's visit next weekend."

"Is something wrong?"

"Besides the usual? No. It's just that we'll probably place top three *this* weekend, and if that happens, we'll need a new routine, and I've been working on something special. Coach isn't making any promises, but she said it doesn't hurt to have more ideas."

"My little multi-tasker. You're growing up so fast."

"So I can skip Dad's?"

I nod. "If he says it's okay with him, then yes, you can skip." If he refused I would step in on her behalf, because sometimes my ex was more focused on appearing to be a good father than actually being one.

Stevie's lip jutted out into an adorable pout that I pretended to be unaffected by. "Fine. And thanks Mom."

"Of course, Stevie. Eat up."

We ate in silence until most of the dinner was agone before Stevie being Stevie, started with more questions. "I read Levi's article in the paper."

Of all the things I expected her to bring up, many of which about Levi, that his article didn't even make the top ten. "You did? Why?"

She shrugged like it was no big deal, but I knew my daughter. "Some of the girls at school have dads like the ones in the article, and they felt inspired by Adrienne's story. And mad. Really, really mad."

I smiled and nodded. "It made me mad too, but it looks like everyone involve is starting to get what they deserve."

"Cool. It's kind of cool having a mom who deals with big issues like that."

"Thank you. Levi did a great job with the story."

Stevie's brows dipped in confusion. "Why didn't you write it Mom? You're a woman."

"Levi is better at writing those kinds of stories because he's been doing it for years."

Stevie nodded. "You should take the next one. Maybe you're just as good or even better than he is, you just don't give yourself enough credit. Like a wise woman once said, you'll never know unless you try." She flashed a toothy, know-it-all grin that made me smile in return.

"Sounds like a very wise woman." Stevie was right, and going forward that would have to be my goal and my attitude. Try and improve with every failure.

My future depended on it.

CHAPTER 16
LEVI

ope to see you tonight.

That message came through from Lacey midday Friday, which surprised me since I hadn't heard from her since that impromptu visit to Michelle's house when she'd grilled me on my career path, and then we'd made out like horny teenagers.

In fact, I hadn't caught but a glimpse of her yesterday, and she hadn't shown up at all on Friday, simply sent a polite and professional email to me and GG saying she was out chasing leads. Chasing leads in Carson Creek, two phrases that didn't seem to go together, which only made me wonder what she was really up to.

"Looking forward to it," I texted back after I got my body and my mind under control. Something about this woman tempted me beyond all reason. I wasn't the man who did relationships, my failure of a marriage and chosen career had proven that time and time again, but here I was in the middle of a secret affair that had me thinking about more.

More of what exactly? I wasn't so sure yet.

But I wanted to explore it, to see what *more* could entail with Lacey.

Lacey's need for secrecy didn't put me off, but after her visit the other night I wondered if it was fear, or something else holding her back and feeding her need for privacy. Then again, it could just be the nosiness of small town living.

"Levi," GG grunted at me about an hour before the day was officially over. The older man was grumpier than usual today and I had a feeling he'd finally picked up on the fact that his daughter was unhappy with him and her career.

"Yeah?"

"Arts and crafts festival this weekend. I need you to cover it." He didn't look up from today's paper and the scowl fixed on his face remained in place.

Arts and crafts festival, words I never thought I'd hear, at least not in terms of a writing assignment. "Sure thing. Is this a well-known event in town?"

GG nodded. "Happens every year, last of the cool weather festivals."

And yet there was no mention of it in the paper and there was no online edition to promote it like crazy. "How do people know about this festival?"

GG looked up at me, his busy brows tugged into a vee of confusion. "It happens every year." The *duh* at the end of that particular sentence went unspoken.

"Right, but it's not on the same weekend or the same dates every year, is it?"

"No. There are signs all over town."

"All right," I sighed because what was the point arguing with a brick wall?

His frown slowly transformed into a satisfied smile now that questioning him was over, and GG nodded. "Good man. Have a good weekend!"

"You heading out?"

He shook his head. "Not for a while, no. Lacey hasn't been in all day and I don't know if she plans on coming in at all today. The paper has to be done for tomorrow's edition."

I bit back a laugh at his complaints. "She wasn't in much yesterday either, but the paper went out, right?"

"Still," he grumbled, muttered under his breath about ungrateful daughters.

Taking the out offered by GG, I shut down my computer, added a reminder about the festival to my phone and straightened my desk. "I'll see you around GG. Have a good weekend."

"Yeah, you too."

I nodded and jogged down the steps that led to the bright and sunny day beyond the brick building. It was a nice afternoon, and I planned to spend a few hours with

Mickey before Michelle's shift ended at the hospital. They had a mother-son date night planned that included a movie and dinner, but it did not include me.

"Go get a life," Michelle had joked, but she still refused to invite me along. "I'm sure Lacey might like to see you tonight." With an eyebrow wiggle, she'd gone back to her books and left it at that.

By the time evening rolled around I was wound so tight I thought I might snap in half. It wasn't just the anticipation of seeing Lacey again, or knowing that I would hold her again, taste her again, hear her melodic laughter again. It was also the simple act of looking forward to seeing another person, a specific person.

I dressed deliberately and added some cologne to the mix before I made my way to the car I rarely used because most places were well within walking distance. I drove to Lacey's place, but I didn't park in front because of privacy, instead I picked an empty spot just a few houses away and killed the engine just as my phone rang.

I smiled at the name on the screen and answered. "Neal, how the hell are you man?"

"Good." I could hear the smile in my old boss' voice. He was a bear of a man with broad shoulders, thick black hair and the smell of tobacco wafting from his entire being. "I saw your story on that lawyer."

"Really?" I knew Lacey promoted it on the paper's

social media pages, but even those didn't have much reach or engagement.

"Yep, damn thing went viral and now the world is talking about women's rights and sexist judges in small towns. Excellent work, my friend." He coughed for a full minute thanks to his favorite vice. "Heard the legislature is calling for an investigation into the named judges."

"Yeah? That's great. I wasn't expecting any of that, but it's a good outcome. She was a very impressive woman, strong and not easily intimidated."

"Can't be, to stand up against a system that's rigged against you and your clients." Neal was impressed by her which was a feat in itself, because nobody impressed him. "You're still doing good work Levi, please tell me you're not satisfied in Podunk America."

I laughed at his nickname for any place that wasn't a city with at least a million residents. "This might surprise you Neal, but I am perfectly happy with my job and my life here in Carson Creek." As I said the words, I realized just how true they were. Of course I wasn't thrilled to cover a small town arts festival, but it was another activity to do with Mickey.

"That's a damn pity."

"Yeah, why is that?" Neal didn't do anything without reason, so I just held my breath and waited.

"Looks like Caracas is burning and Venezuela is on the brink of civil war thanks to the failing economy and the new government. Thought you might be interested in the story. Guess I was wrong." Neal let the words linger in the air, allowing the weight of the situation to sink in the way he always did as he waited for me to agree, the way I always did.

Always.

"You are wrong," I told him. "Sorry, but I can't fly off to Venezuela right now, but I think maybe I have someone in mind."

"Yeah? Well I'll touch base with you again in a day or two as the situation changes. Let me know." Neal ended the call before I could say anything else, his way of letting the story burrow deep in my mind until I packed my bags and hopped a flight to the next world shit show.

I took a moment, possibly two, to talk myself out of doing just that, reminding myself that I had commitments here in town. Mickey needed me and we had plans for the coming weeks and months, I couldn't leave. I wouldn't.

Didn't even want to.

I had Mickey and Michelle to think about.

And Lacey.

Lacey. Just the thought of her made me smile and cleared all thoughts of a new story from my mind as I stepped from the car and strolled casually to her front door.

Lacey opened the door with a sexy, welcoming smile

that quickly died on her lips. "What's wrong Levi? Is Mickey okay? Michelle?"

I smiled at her concern but it wasn't a real smile, more like an affectionate grin. " It's nothing," I told her a bit too easily.

"Don't start lying to me now Levi." She put one hand on her hip and motioned me inside with the other, a scowl on her face. "Just tell me what's bothering you."

"It's nothing. Really."

"Yeah? Then I must be losing my touch if I invite a man over for a hot meal and even hotter sex, and he shows up frowning."

"Lacey," I sighed because it wasn't fair to let her think she had anything to do with it.

"Don't give me excuses Levi, just give me the truth while I make you a stiff drink."

Without waiting for my agreement, Lacey headed towards the kitchen and the most delightful smells blended with her floral perfume, intoxicating me as I entered. "I don't need a stiff drink," I assured her as she reached for a bottle in the freezer.

"Well that's too bad." She turned to me with a sweet smile. "Because you've got one, and it's strong enough to loosen that talented tongue of yours."

I smiled at her and took the drink. "Thanks." The whiskey was ice cold as I sipped it, and it started to work immediately. "It's silly," I said and launched into Neal's offer. "I turned him down right away, but this is the first time an opportunity has presented itself, and it feels strange to walk away from a story like that. But I did it, I said no and I meant it."

Lacey stared at me, head tilted with an affectionate grin. "It feels like a loss because now it's real. You put your family first instead of the story."

"Yeah," I growled and took a long gulp of the cold liquid.

"If you're not ready to step away completely, we can make it work. This is Carson Creek after all, we take care of our own, and I'm sure between me and Valona and plenty of others in town, we can take care of Mickey for a week or two."

Her words stole the breath from my lungs and I smiled at her like a fool. "You don't know how much I appreciate the offer, Lacey. Hell you don't know how sexy it is that you understand enough to make the offer."

"Yeah, you're turned on by babysitting offers?" She wiggled her eyebrows and laughed, and that little move lifted the weight off my shoulders a little more.

"I think it's generous, beautiful blonds," I shot back with a smile that faded. "Michelle wouldn't understand, she would just see the same old pattern, and she wouldn't be wrong Lacey."

"So you're staying but you're going to be miserable about it."

"No, not miserable. It was just a shock, that's all," I assure her because the more I talked about it with her, the less it felt like a sacrifice. "That call was just a reminder, a very real one, in fact. That's not my life anymore, which is odd sure, but I'm not sad about it."

"No?"

I shook my head. "It's like dieting, the big victories come when you resist temptation, not the days you simply do the right thing. I got the offer and turned it down, which was me making the choice to stay here."

Lacey stood, and I thought maybe the conversation had ruined the mood for the evening, but she walked around the table and sat in my lap, wrapping her arms around me and squeezing tight.

"I'm proud of you Levi. I know how hard that must have been, but you chose Michelle and Mickey. That's huge."

"Thank you."

"Thank *you* for reminding me that there are still good men in the world." She lowered her head until our lips touched and flames exploded all around us. The kiss started as an inferno, lips and tongues touched, licked, nipped and tasted with the kind of wild abandon usually reserved for long lost lovers. She kissed me and I kissed her, chests heaving, breaths sawing in and out when we pulled apart and stared at each other in awe. In disbelief.

"Wow." Lacey's blue eyes were nearly black with desire, lips swollen from my kisses, cheeks a little scraped from my stubble. "Levi," she moaned and put her lips to mine again, hungrier and hotter than the first kiss.

It was unlike anything I had ever experienced, this kind of intense passion, especially in the wake of such a serious conversation. But the longer our mouths fused, the more I wanted it. The more I wanted this woman.

"Lacey," I growled against her mouth and stood.

Her head fell back, giving me full access to her graceful neck and I took full advantage, nibbling my way up to her chin and across her jawline before I kissed my way to her collarbone while she writhed in my arms. The plan had been to take her to the bedroom, but the inviting rug in front of the coffee table was perfect.

Just perfect.

I laid her down on the rug and stared down at her beautiful, flushed face, nipples hard through the thin cotton fabric of another one of those shirt dresses she loved so much. I was starting to love them too.

"Levi, I need you. Please."

It wasn't elegant or beautiful, the hungry, frenetic way we came together right there on the floor, but it was so intense my skin flamed with heat. I undressed her quickly, teasing only enough to make her squirm. "You are so damn beautiful."

"I'm just me," she whispered and tangled her fingers in my hair as my lips nibbled hers, her chin, her throat and down to that heated space between her gorgeous breasts. Lacey didn't know how beautiful, how appealing she was, and that only made me more determined to show her.

"Just you is more than enough," I assured her as I slipped my shoulders between her thighs to flick my tongue over the swollen nub peeking between her folds.

"Levi!" Her hips bucked off the floor and I tugged her clit between my lips and sucked. Hard. "Oh, Levi." Her chest heaved, her fingers tightened around my locks and she growled.

I made Lacey Gregory growl, and next I was determined to make her mine.

"Levi," She growled again. "No more. I need you. You. Now."

Those words were the only ones that could have pulled me from her sweet nectar, the naked need in her tone and it was all for me. I could barely breathe when I looked down at her, completely naked and turned on. "Now?"

She nodded. "Right now." Lacey was on her knees in front of me, helping me rid myself of the clothes that stood between us. Her fingers moved quickly to remove my pants and boxers in one quick shove down my hips. Her lips quirked into a hungry smile when she freed my erection and as I watched, unable to look away as she took me in her hands and then her mouth.

"Lacey." That was as far as I got before her lush lips and hot mouth took me in and sent me to heaven. Her mouth was as talented as she'd accused mine of being, and watching her only heightened my desire and took me closer to the edge. She took me deep and swallowed around me. My eyes closed and my jaw clenched as I fought for control. But Lacey did it again and all thoughts of control fled.

My hips bucked twice and she didn't flinch as she took me deeper with a low moan.

"God, woman." I pulled away and used the length of my body to take us both to the ground, settling on top of her and sliding deep in one long, slow move. "You undo me, Lacey."

She smiled up at me and wrapped her legs around my waist, urging me deeper. I gave her exactly what she wanted, what we both wanted more than we wanted our next breath. She moaned and gasped, cried my name when I hit that spot she loved.

"Levi, oh god Levi." Her head shot back, eyes fluttered closed and her back arched.

Gorgeous. I leaned forward unable to wait another minute to taste her again, tugging a nipple between my teeth as I took her a hundred miles past the summit and together, we fell.

I don't know how long we floated like that, bodies shaking and trembling with pleasure, gazes locked on one another like magnets. Eventually, maybe an eternity later, we landed back on that rug in her living room, smiling like fools and gasping for air. "What was that?"

Her question shocked a laugh out of me. "If you have

to ask, maybe we need to do again to refresh your recollection."

It was her turn to laugh. "Sure. As. Soon. As. I. Can. Breathe. Again."

I kissed her again, long and slow, enjoying the tight pulsing clench of her body around mine, the aftershocks that shook her. "Have you caught your breath yet?"

She laughed and I rolled to my side, bringing her with me so I could look into her blue eyes, her smiling face. "I don't know Levi, you kind of take my breath away."

Exactly the words I wanted to hear from this woman. "Good to know." I pressed another kiss to her lips and pulled back, my head propped on my hand as I watched her closely, accepted the fact that I was falling hard for this woman without knowing how she truly felt. "I have an idea."

"Naked dinner?"

I laughed. "I'll leave that decision up to the hostess. About Venezuela."

Lacey's body went stiff, but her expression never changed. "I'm listening."

"Maybe this can be your first big international story for your new venture. It's guaranteed to be a great story with national headlines that will put you on the map."

The smile she sent me, like I was some kind of hero, made me uncomfortable. I wasn't a hero. A real hero wouldn't have even thought, for one moment, about breaking his promise and leaving his family behind, for another story. Her smile widened and Lacey sat up close, her forehead right against mine. "You really think I could do it?"

I nodded. "Absolutely. You're tough, strong, determined and stubborn as hell. Crucial tools for any crisis journalist." She leaned in and kissed me, and I wondered if I screwed up. Did she think I was trying to get her out of town for a while?

Her eyelashes fluttered when she pulled back, plump lips slowly forming into a smile. "I'll think about it."

"Good."

"But for now," she pushed at my chest until I was flat on my back. "Now, I've caught my breath Levi."

And I spent the next hour stealing it all back. Twice.

CHAPTER 17
LACEY

"I'm telling you Pippa, nothing can ruin this day. Nothing at all." It was late on Saturday as I drove back from day one of Stevie's cheerleading competition, muscles still deliciously sore from the most fantastic Friday in the history of Friday nights.

My sister-in-law laughed, and I could just picture her in the backyard with a glass of sweet tea, feet propped up with her free hand rubbing her swollen belly. "You know saying that is like tempting fate. In the restaurant business we never say, 'it's a quiet night' or 'it's dead in here' because statements like that inevitably lead to a packed house."

"It's a good thing I'm not superstitious," I reminded her with a smile as I made my way to the CCDJ offices to prep tomorrow's edition.

"How did Stevie's squad do today?"

"Second place overall, so they're busy tonight practicing stunts and over obsessing about tomorrow." Stevie had been so excited to see me in the stands cheering her on that it was well worth the lack of sleep to make the two and a half hour drive to watch my baby girl perform. "Tomorrow will determine if they go to nationals."

"So exciting," Pippa sighed. "You finally got laid," she said after a long pregnant pause.

"Says who?"

"Um, the over the top cheerfulness you're displaying for one," she said around a laugh. "Those little swoony sighs of yours, which I'm sure have to do with a certain ruggedly hot newspaper man."

"Fine," I admitted. "But it wasn't the first time."

"What? You've been holding out on me? What a bad sister-in-law you are!"

I laughed and unlocked the glass door before I made my way upstairs. "It's a secret sort of thing for now, you know how gossip can be." Levi was just for me, at least for now anyway. I didn't have to share him or our activities with anyone else.

"How long do you plan to keep it from the world?"

I shrugged even though Pippa couldn't see me. "I don't know. Right now we work together, which doesn't look good. And we don't know what this is, or if it's going to be anything. It's too new for Carson Creek scrutiny."

"If you're sure," she shot back in a sing-song voice that made me wonder if I was really sure.

"I'm not, but I will be. I'm at the office now Pip, gotta go. Talk later." I had a few hours left to go over the stories that would appear in tomorrow's paper, adjust the layout if necessary and get it off to the printers, but there was more than enough time to get the Sunday edition delivered by the crack of dawn.

"This conversation isn't over Lacey, just paused. For now." Pippa ended the call and I couldn't help but smile at her bossy tone.

The front page story would, of course, be the Arts and Crafts Festival because it was what was considered front page news for Daddy. I even included a photo of Mickey making a mess of the hand churned ice cream that was always a big hit at every festival in town. Instead of following up the feel-good front page story with more fluff though, I added the small piece I'd written about the recall election of one of the judges from Levi's story on Adrienne. It was a good balance, and even though I knew GG would yell down the house tomorrow, I did it anyway.

"So, you *do* still work here." GG's disgruntled voice came from right behind me and I let out a startled gasp.

"Did you think a ghost was putting the paper together each day?" A man who loved to complain would always find a reason to do so, even if no legitimate reason existed.

"How would I know when you haven't been to the office in days?" He was in a mood to fight, and I wasn't.

But Pippa's warning from earlier rang in my head. I jinxed myself by proclaiming that nothing could ruin the day. "I have been in, that's how come the paper still goes out each day. Unless you thought it magically put itself together and off to the printer's each night?"

"Don't be a smart ass."

"Don't say things just to make me mad. You sound like a grumpy old man." I arranged and re-arranged the inside pages to make sure the necessary ads fit around the stories with the promised size margins. "What are you doing here?"

"Came to put the paper to bed."

I rolled my eyes and kept my comments to myself. *I am not going to argue with him. Not tonight.* GG hadn't put the paper to bed in well over a decade, because I was here every single night to do it. There were no vacations for me, no weekends away, just a few hours here and there to myself.

"That's not right," he pointed to the ad. "They always get the long banner style ad." He tapped his finger on my screen.

"No, they *usually* get the banner ad. For this edition they got the postcard style."

"That can't be right." GG shook his head and leaned over my shoulder until his face was mere inches from the screen. "You sure?"

I bit my tongue so hard I thought it might start to bleed. "Feel free to pull up the ad buys for the Sunday edition and check for yourself."

He shuffled off to do just that, because suddenly I didn't know how to do the same job I've been doing since I was a girl. My anger grew and I worked faster, determined to get this done before GG returned with more complaints. "I guess you were right," he conceded reluctantly.

I kept my eyes on the layout until it was complete. I sat back and scrolled through everything one final time just as I felt the heat of my father against my back.

His finger slid over my shoulder and he pressed it right against the screen. Again. It was a small thing, just one more piece of evidence that he didn't value me, my hard work or my opinion. "We're not putting this on the front page, Lacey. How many damn times do I have to tell you?" He shook his head. "Stupid, stubborn girl."

His words were like a punch to the gut and I reared back. "Excuse me?"

He shook his head. "I've told you time and again, nothing serious on the front pages. What the hell is wrong with you girl?"

"I am not a girl!" Roaring the words probably wasn't the best way to get my point across, then again nothing would get the point across. I was a forty-five year old, divorced single mother, and still, all he saw was a little girl incapable of doing anything. "You know what

Daddy? You know how to do this, and you do it better than anyone else in the whole entire world, so why don't you just do it yourself. That way each day you can rest easy knowing that *your* precious paper is done to your standards." I stood and gathered my things, picking up half a dozen photos of me and Stevie, me and my brothers, Stevie and her uncles, and shoved them in my bag.

"Don't be dramatic, girl. I'm just trying to teach you how to do things the right way."

"No, you just want things done your way, the same way things have been done for fifty years."

"Damn right, and it's been working for the past fifty years. It would be nice to see it go for another fifty," he shot back, his implication clear.

"Good luck to you Daddy. I'm out of here and I'm not coming back." I pulled out each drawer, one by one, and removed every personal item that had gathered over the years from hair bands to magnets, a stray Christmas ornament, notes and more photos.

"You're not going anywhere, Lacey. Where will you go? What will you do?"

"Don't act like you care now, Daddy. You have the thing you care about most, this paper. Enjoy it." With my bag bursting at the seams, I glared at my father, turned on my heels and stormed off in a cloud of fury all Hollywood actresses would envy.

I was too angry to go home to an empty house, too wound up to just pace the living room with a glass of wine, but I had nowhere to go. It was too late to disturb Pippa, even though she would welcome me with open arms.

Levi.

His name came to me and instantly I knew, he was who I wanted, who I needed in the moment. It was late, but not indecently late, so I drove to his place and sat in my car for five minutes before I gathered the courage to go to his door.

"Lacey, hey." His voice was low and unsure.

I took a step back. "I'm sorry. I shouldn't have come here. It's late and you're busy."

Levi's hand shot out to grab my wrist before I could take another step back. "What's wrong?"

"Nothing," I shook my head.

His lips curled into a lopsided grin. "Don't go lying to me now Lacey." He tossed my words back in my face and dammit, it irked. "Come in and tell me what's wrong."

I let him tug me inside, surprised to see the television off with papers scattered on the coffee table. "You're busy, Levi."

"Not too busy for you. Just outlining a story on some of the vendors at the festival." He clasped his hand with mine and led me to the kitchen. "What's going on?"

"I quit." I ignored the stab of pain in my chest as the words rushed out of me.

"You quit CCDJ?"

I nodded. "Yes. Just now, in fact."

Sympathy flashed in his eyes and Levi turned to the fridge, reaching on top for a bottle. "It's not whiskey and it's not cold, but according to Michelle tequila can fix nearly all ails, and she's a doctor so you can trust her."

I laughed and accepted the shot with a smile of gratitude. "GG came in acting like I was shirking my duties because he hadn't seen me in the office. I mean, how else is the paper getting out every day? Every single day," I growled and knocked back the shot.

"I'm sorry it didn't feel as good as you thought, Lacey." His strong arms wrapped around me in a tight, enveloping hug. "It'll get better."

"I know," I sighed into his chest. "I know I did the right thing, I just hate that he pushed it like that." Tears started to sting my eyes and I blinked them away.

"It's all right to be emotional about it. This is the end of a dream, of a future you thought was all but guaranteed. That's sad, also maddening."

"Right?" It was nice to know someone else understood that this wasn't about my ego. "I am mad," I admitted and knocked the bottom of the shot against the kitchen table to ask for more. "I put my own dreams on hold, stayed here and settled down because Daddy promised I would run the paper someday. He was never going to let me run it." My shoulders sank and my head fell forward as sadness swamped me. "Never."

He poured another shot and then Levi's big warm

hand rubbed circles against my back as the tears streamed down my cheeks, and small sobs shook me. "If it makes you feel better, I don't think his behavior has much to do with you."

I sat back and stared at him. "How could it not? It's me he's deemed incompetent to run the paper. He thinks I'll screw it all up and ruin his legacy."

"Hardly. Has GG always behaved this way towards you?"

I thought about it and I was forced to admit that he used to be supportive and kind, almost professional. "No, just the last few years."

"Because he's not ready to give up being GG the Newspaper Man, so he's looking for reasons to stay relevant, to make sure he's still needed."

There was some logic to Levi's words, but I wasn't in the mood to hear it or to have any sympathy for Daddy. "All at the expense of my confidence? Sorry Levi, I don't care."

"I'm not asking you to care, I'm just telling you that you're a good editor and you're doing a great job running CCDJ. Don't let an old man's inability to let go make you doubt that."

I smiled at him. "You're really sweet, you know that?" He was a good man with great insight and for now, he was here with me.

"Sweet? That's a first for me, but I'll take your word for it."

"It's true. You have a way with people, and I can see why your career is so incredible. You see people and you understand them, it's your superpower."

His smile was seductive. "And here I was thinking something else was my superpower."

"Well, that's definitely a superpower, without a doubt, but I don't think that's something the whole world needs to know about."

He flashed another smile that was pure mischief, and I knew in that moment that I was falling for this man. It wasn't just the earth shattering sex or that he was a great listener, it was everything about him, from his love of wool socks and checkered shirts to his playful smile and dancing eyes. "That, is just for you Lacey."

"Good to know." I smiled up at him like a giddy girl, and that's exactly how I felt. Giddy and warm with affection. "I've already bought a domain and hired a designer for my new venture, Carson Creek Online. I'll be ready with the first stories in about two weeks."

"Really? That's great Lacey." His smile was genuine. "I knew you were up to something, but I didn't know what."

"I wasn't sure if I could even do it, and honestly I'm still not sure, but it's now or never, right?" At least I hoped so. "And if you have any stories you want published that aren't right for CCDJ, you know where to find me to convince me."

"Well, now you're just making sure I write something that I have to convince you is worth publishing." He was playful and flirty, and I loved this side of him as much as the serious side.

"If you think that's what you have to do, go for it." I laughed, and for the first time since my blow up with Daddy, I felt good, as if I could actually do this and succeed. As if maybe this might be my calling instead of running a local newspaper.

"I would start on the convincing now, but Mickey is a light sleeper and you're not exactly quiet."

I felt heat suffuse my cheeks at his words and I sat up taller, chin high in the air. "Technically that's your fault, not mine."

Levi's smile faded and his hand fell to my thigh and squeezed. "That sounds like a challenge. First one to make a sound loses?" His gaze was mischievous, his lips teasing a smile. "What do you say Lacey?"

I smiled at him and put my hand on top of his. "I say give it your best shot Levi. I don't like to lose."

He grinned and leaned forward until his lips brushed against mine. "In that case I'll just say this up front, I'm sorry for your loss." Laughter bubbled out of me at the same time his lips captured mine and he kissed me until I was breathless and dizzy, and begging for more.

Needless to say, I accepted his apology with grace.

And a very satisfied smile.

CHAPTER 18
LEVI

"You want me to go down to Venezuela? With a newbie? With a civil war on the horizon?" One of my oldest friends, Carlton Linelli, laughed down the line at my apparently absurd question. "Seriously Levi, what's going on? Has small town living rotted your brain?"

I rolled my eyes and pinched the bridge of my nose. "Thinking more clearly than I have in twenty years. Can you do this for me? I'd consider it a favor to be repaid at a later date."

The laughter died and Carlton sighed thoughtfully. "You're serious."

"I am. This is a big opportunity, and only the best will make me happy." I'd been trying for days to arrange things for this Venezuela trip, and it was just about set. "It shouldn't take longer than a week."

When he sighed, I knew I had him. "You know I can't turn down a trip, and I get to show off my tan biceps."

I laughed. "That won't be necessary, keep your bulging muscles to yourself please."

"Oh, it's like that, is it?"

I smiled. "No, just this trip is important. That's all."

"Fine, I'm in. Email me the details."

I flashed a triumphant smile and pumped my fist in the air. I loved it when a plan came together flawlessly. "Thanks Carl, I owe you one."

"And don't you forget it," he grunted. "I have a date to get ready for, with a model. I'll be looking for those details."

"I'll send them over now," I assured him and ended the call.

"You're leaving." Michelle's voice startled me, and I turned to see her arms crossed, face twisted into a frown. "I guess giving me enough notice to make plans for your absence was too much to ask?"

"Michelle." My shoulders fell at her anger, her insinuation. "I've been here for months, helping with Mickey and trying to make your life easier and still you don't trust me?" It hurt, but I knew I'd done this to her, to us.

"Trust takes time, and a few months, while appreciated, isn't near long enough to forget a lifetime of packed bags and rushed goodbyes."

"I know and I'm sorry, but I can't change that Michelle. I've apologized and I showed up here when you needed me to do more than just *say* that I'm sorry. What more can I do?" I started to have a deeper understanding of Lacey's problems with GG in that moment. Would my actions today ever make up for the past?

"You can start by not rushing off at the first sign of problems in the world, Dad."

I nodded. "I deserve that, and I know it, but this time you're wrong."

My daughter, as stubborn as I was, tightened her arms around herself and lifted her chin high in the air, a smug look on her face. "So that wasn't Saul with another assignment that you *just can't* pass up halfway around the world?"

I grinned at her words, a sad grin that served as a reminder of the damage my actions had caused. "No, smartass. It was Carlton."

Her face paled. "So, the trip is booked already and you really are leaving." The air deflated out of her and she dropped down on the sofa. "I'm actually surprised."

That cheered me up some. "Good. It means you're starting to trust me, to take me at my word."

"Fat lot of good that's doing for me at the moment." Her shoulders sank in disappointment, and I could see the gears churning in her head, thinking of who she could call to fill in as Mickey's full-time caregiver.

"I'm not going to Venezuela, Michelle."

"It's all right Dad, I get it."

"No, you really don't. I called Carlton because I need

someone I trust to go with Lacey to Venezuela. If I can convince her to do this story."

She looked up at me with wide eyes, filled with shock. "What? Really?"

I flashed a soft smile and nodded. "Lacey is ready to do this, and more importantly I think this story and this experience will be good for her. Saul wanted me to go with her, but I don't want to step on her toes or overshadow her."

"That's why this is important? Because of Lacey?" Michelle's smile came slowly, a hint of mischief behind it. "You must really care about Lacey."

"I do." I cared about Lacey more than I'd cared about my wife, which was either romantic or pathetic.

"You never turned down a story for me." The words were said without a hint of malice or accusation, just stated as a cold hard fact, which I could appreciate.

"No, I didn't, and I'm sorry as hell for that. But being here with you and Mickey, it's taught me how to be better for the people I care about. I'm sorry I didn't learn that when it would have meant something to you, Michelle."

"I know."

"I turned down this story for you, not Lacey. Well, for Mickey too." I smiled at the idea that the best part of my day was hanging out with a toddler. "I gave you my word and I meant it. With all of my heart. I just wish it meant something to you."

"It does," she sighed and shook her head. "When it comes to you Dad, I am incapable of being the calm and cool Dr. Branson, I'm just little Shellie Branson, wishing her daddy would show up for science fair, debate club and all the other things I did to get your attention."

"Well, you have it now, if that helps." I pulled Michelle out of her chair and did the thing I should have done each time I returned home from a trip, I wrapped her in my arms and squeezed her tight.

"It does." She hugged me back and buried her face in my chest.

"Good, because if I could go back in time and do it all over again, I would do things differently. Being here with Mickey makes it real, all the things I missed out on with you, the things I chalked up to insignificant events to be made up for at a later date. I can never get that time back with you, and I'm sorry for that, but I'm grateful to you for giving me a second chance, and a chance to fall in love with the greatest little boy on earth. For letting me see all that I missed with you."

Michelle laughed and pulled back, shaking her head in amusement. "Mickey loves you, and that more than makes up for everything, especially since his dad is such a loser." She sighed as if she had the weight of the world on her shoulders. "He doesn't even have some amazing job as a reason for being a shit dad." She winced at her insinuation. "Sorry."

"Don't be. Facts are always fact, even when they sting."

"I know, but I shouldn't keep coming at you like that."

"Maybe you should. And trust me when I tell you that there is no good reason for being a shit dad."

Michelle's arms slid around my waist and she hugged me again. "I love you, Daddy."

"Love you too, sweetheart." I squeezed her tight. "I am so proud of the woman you've become, achieving so much on your own."

She giggled and pulled back, a knowing smile lit up her face. "You also love Lacey, so much that you gave her a big story. A really big story, I'm guessing."

I growled and ruffled her hair, enjoying her squeal of outrage. "Let's not talk about that right now."

"Okay, fine, but you can't avoid this forever. You know that, right?"

I nodded. "Yeah, I know. Not forever, but maybe for just a little while longer." I couldn't tell Lacey now, not when she was about to get the chance to have the career she'd always wanted. There would be time later.

I hoped so at least.

CHAPTER 19
LACEY

"And then Coach Matthews said she wants to use my whole entire routine for the next tournament! Can you believe it, Mom?" Stevie's eyes rolled back and she shook her head and stomped her feet with excitement. "I'm totally having a fit right now."

I couldn't help but smile at the joy that radiated from my daughter. The divorce was hard on her, harder on her than on me, and to see her finding joy in her favorite hobbies and activities warmed my heart. She'd returned to the happy little girl she was before her father tossed us aside.

"You can't see it, but I'm also totally having a fit right now."

"Mom," she groaned.

"Seriously, I am so proud of you Stevie. I can't wait to

see your choreography." Now that I worked for myself, I could actually grab my laptop and work while all the other teams performed, I could support her the way a mother should. I could buy her and team a meal after a job well done because I didn't have to rush back to Carson Creek to put the paper to bed.

"Thanks Mom, I'm pretty proud too." She pointed at her math textbook. "That's why I'm getting my homework done before dinner, so I can break down the steps to teach the girls. Regionals are just a few weeks away."

"That's my girl," I told her just as the phone rang. "Hello?"

"Lacey Gregory?" The voice was deep, very deep and slightly accented.

"This is Lacey, who is this?"

"The name is Carlton, but you can call me Carl since we'll be spending a week together in South America." His voice was filled with amusement, and I frowned.

"I'm sorry, but I think you have the wrong Lacey Gregory."

"Nope, don't think so."

He laughed, and the sound was rich and smooth, like he used that masculine laugh often. "I talked to Levi yesterday and he said you were in need of a cameraman, which I am. I do stills and video, oh and I'm fluent in Spanish if that helps."

I stared at my phone in disbelief, at the conversation I was having. "It does help, but I'm really not sure what you're talking about, or why Levi told you I needed a cameraman." Had I hit my head and woken up in an alternate dimension?

The doorbell rang and Stevie perked up, eyes filled with curiosity. "I'll get it."

"For Venezuela."

"Venezuela?"

"Yep. When do you want to leave? I have another job hanging open until I nail down these dates."

My head was spinning. "I'm sorry, but I'm really confused right now."

Stevie returned to the kitchen with a knowing smile as Levi entered behind her. "It's Levi," she said in a sing-song voice.

"Carlton? Levi has just showed up in my kitchen, so when I know what's going on I promise to call you back."

"All right," he sighed, amusement highlighting his tone. "Tell Levi I said *I knew it*."

"Uh, I will, and thank you for keeping these dates open for me?"

He laughed. "Talk to you soon Lacey."

The call ended and I stared at Levi, ruggedly handsome in a blue and green checkered shirt, jeans that fit a little snug, and casual boots that painted him as a Carson Creek native.

"Want to tell me what's going on?"

He smiled down at me and I felt that smile all the

way down to my soul. "I have a plan. Remember I told you about the civil unrest in Venezuela?" I nodded, brows still furrowed in confusion. "Well, I think this is the perfect story for you to get your feet wet as a journalist on location."

"What?" I couldn't believe the words that were coming out of his mouth. "Me? I'm a small town journalist, Levi."

"No, you *were* a small town journalist. You haven't told me everything, or much of anything about your future plans, but I am more than just a pretty face, you know?"

"You're also a cute butt."

"Gross," Stevie grumbled behind Levi.

"Think of the experience, Lacey. Reporting a story on the ground as it happens. And best of all, you can post the stories as they happen."

I sucked in a breath. "How did you know?"

"Because you were never going to leave Carson Creek while Stevie's having the best cheerleading season of her life."

"Totally," my nosy daughter agreed.

"None of that matters, what matters is if you want this Lacey."

My heart kicked up a notch, pounding against my chest like I'd just run circles around Carson Creek. "I do, Levi. I want it badly, but I'm not ready for boots on the ground reporting."

He chuckled, the sound smooth and rich like a good scotch. "You'll never be ready until you are, and when you get there, you will be ready." His smile was so encouraging I started to believe him.

"I don't know, Levi. South America is a long way from here."

"Which is why you need to be there to tell this story. It's a story the world will want to know about, and you can tell them why it's important and why they should care." He gave my shoulders a tight squeeze. "Carlton is the best, and he speaks Spanish which will help you get access to people to interview. You've got a long flight to research the situation and figure out how you want tell the story."

He'd thought of everything. Had an answer for my every objection. Levi Branson could be my perfect man. Emphasis on *could be*. "You really are sweet as pie for a hardened world-weary investigative journalist."

The smile he sent me came slow and sexy. "That's because I've got layers, babe."

"All right, that's it." Stevie slammed her text book shut and pushed away from the counter. "You guys are totally gross and kind of sweet for old people, but it's too much." Her smile softened her harsh words. "And Mom, this is totally an amazing opportunity. Super cool, and I think you should do it. I'll even volunteer to spend the week with Dad so you have no excuse not to go."

"Thanks honey."

"No problem. I'm going now, so you guys can totally kiss," she shouted as she made her way up the stairs in dramatic fashion, making as much noise as possible until her door closed with an almost inaudible click.

Levi pulled me in close, his hands on my hips, his gaze fixed on me. Only me. "You can thank me properly now."

I tilted my head back and laughed. And then I got down to the very important business of thanking Levi.

Properly.

CHAPTER 20
LEVI

The Carson Creek Daily Journal offices were a lot quieter without the presence of Lacey, who always managed to find a way to make noise. To make her presence known. Whether it was humming, the low rock-country music she often sang along to, the buzz of the printer or just the *tap-tap-tap* of her fingers flying across the keyboard, she was impossible to ignore. Without her, the office was deathly silent. Lifeless.

Even GG seemed to be affected by the loss he likely hadn't truly believed was coming until one day passed without her, and then the next. The old man would never admit it, because he was from the old school where men kept their emotions hidden no matter what. Still, every car that drove past the office made him look up. When someone came in for an ad, he looked up with hope in his eyes that only faded when he realized it wasn't his beloved daughter.

"This damn thing," he grumbled from Lacey's office, and I grinned.

GG was a lot of things, but young with a good memory he was not. He might have worked in this office for decades, but he'd forgotten a lot more about the day to day running of a newspaper than he remembered. "Everything all right, GG?"

"Hell no, it ain't all right," he growled. A beat later his head popped out of Lacey's office, mussed silver hair leading the way. "You know anything about putting a paper to bed?"

"Nope," I told him. "Never worked in a traditional office until now." And I had no real desire to learn something that was becoming more and more irrelevant with every passing day.

"Never?"

I shrugged. "I ran errands and transcribed notes for reporters in high school and did a semester at the college paper, but that's about it."

His lips pulled into a hopeful grin. "Want to learn?"

"Nah." I shook my head and bit back a grin. "You're awfully particular about how you want it all done, so I would think it'd be a treat for you to get reacquainted with the process."

"Smart ass," he murmured and disappeared into the office again. I couldn't tell if he was trying to put the paper to bed, or redecorate Lacey's office with the noises that came from that direction, so I kept my attention on the laptop screen and the stories I had to write before tomorrow. "Don't think you and Lacey are foolin' anyone, either." GG's tone was annoyed and slightly distracted. "It doesn't take a genius to figure out really, but I've never claimed to be a genius so why don't you tell me what's going on in my daughter's head?"

I thought long and hard about what I should and would say before I answered. GG cared about his daughter, but he was also a proud man who would never admit his shortcomings. I sighed and leaned back with my feet propped up on my desk. "You mean other than the fact that you seem to think she's incompetent? My guess is nothing."

"What? That's nonsense, Lacey is brilliant and she's the most capable person I know."

His words even shocked me, and I shook my head. "That may be what's in your heart, but I have to tell you GG, that's not obvious from your words or your actions."

"Hogwash," he grumbled and swatted a dismissive hand in my direction. "I just want to make sure she's ready for the responsibility of running a paper. It's not easy, the job or the life."

That's what he *thought* he was doing. "Seems like you want her to run the paper exactly the way you have all these years without making any changes."

"What's wrong with how I run things? This is what

put food on the table for four kids and paid off a nice family home."

"There's nothing wrong with it GG, but do you know about all the changes in news media over the past twenty years?"

"I know what I need to know."

"Yeah, and it worked for you, but how is Lacey supposed to compete in this new world?" I shook my head. "This is exactly why family businesses don't often last but two or three generations. The older generations don't want to keep up with the times and Lacey doesn't want to work in the past."

"Did she tell you that?"

"She didn't have to. I have eyes and ears, GG. And I've been around the block a time or two, worked for owners who proclaimed the internet a fad until they owned dying newspapers."

GG aimed an angry finger in my direction. "That's not going to happen with this newspaper."

"You hope," I added with a smile.

"You think I'm too hard on Lacey, don't you?"

"No, I think you have a hard time treating her like a grown woman. You still treat her the way you did when she started working at your side in high school. I think you don't respect her or her ideas, and I'm guessing that's close to what she thinks. But I can't speak for Lacey, so maybe you should talk to her."

GG nodded and stared at the carpet for a long time,

saying nothing. "I'll talk to her. I'll apologize when she gets over her mad and comes back to the office."

"And if she doesn't?"

"She will," he said, more to himself than to me. "She will."

I didn't know how to tell him that pigs would fly before Lacey came back, and thankfully my alarm to pick up Mickey went off, so I didn't have to tell the old man the harsh truth.

CHAPTER 21
LACEY

My site was live. Officially. I stared at the screen with a big goofy grin. It was a bare bones site for now, with just a few stories published by me and a few more pulled from the news wires. It wasn't much right now, but it was a start.

A good, if underwhelming start.

The past few days had been incredibly busy between research and packing for my trip, not to mention getting Carson Creek Online up and generating traffic before heading off to a potential civil war. I'd barely had any time to just sit and think. About leaving Stevie with her father for a week. About how Daddy was doing at the paper without me. About Levi, and getting naked with Levi, and being wrapped in his arms. About South America.

There were too many thoughts flying around my

head to sit on one for any length of time, mostly because I was terrified of what came next. What if Venezuela was a flop? What if Carson Creek Online was a flop? For all my supposed courage and bravado, I was terrified that I wouldn't be able to do it, at least not as well as Levi had for decades.

I had an idea how the story might go, but I refused to fence myself in to one particular narrative until I was able to talk to the people most affected by what has already happened, and what might happen next.

After three hours of staring at the screen and making small tweaks here, double checking facts there, I sat back and let out an exhausted breath. Researching this story was, somehow, even harder work than one full day at CCDJ.

"Dream big, they said. You'll be rewarded, they said." I was equally excited and anxious about Venezuela, mostly about my success or failure, because Levi had assured me that Carlton was a man he trusted with his life on dozens of occasions.

The doorbell rang and I frowned. It was the middle of a workday, so this was unexpected. On the other side of the door was Pippa looking fifty months pregnant, and my brother Ryan who glowered beside her. "Hey guys, what's up?"

"What's up," Ryan growled, his face twisted into an angry scowl. "What's up is that you quit on Daddy."

"First of all, watch your tone. Second of all, I didn't

quit on our father, I quit a job on my boss who did not appreciate me or the work I put into help his business succeed."

"*His* business? That's the family business Lacey."

"Yeah? Really? Because I don't see any other family working there." I shook my head in the face of my brother's anger. "Look, if you care so much about the paper all of a sudden, you go work at Daddy's side."

That took some of the steam out of his sails. "You love working at the paper."

I nodded. "I used to. It was my favorite thing in the world, but that's the past, and if you can't handle that, you can leave."

"I'm not going anywhere, dammit."

"Then I guess that means you can either be happy for me, or keep your mouth shut." I loved my brothers, truly I did, but they drove me crazy at the same time.

"Be happy?" He looked around the freshly cleaned living room and shrugged. "That you're out of work?"

"You think the only person who would hire me is my own father? Great to know what you think of me, Ryan." I always suspected my brothers thought I stayed in Carson Creek because I couldn't hack it out in the world, but now I knew for sure.

"Lacey, that's not what I meant." He raked a hand through his thick hair and blew out a frustrated breath, but I ignored him and turned to Pippa.

"How are you feeling, Pippa?"

Her smile brightened. "I'm great. Exhausted, and I have to pee all the time, but I can't complain. Other than, you know, this fighting." Her gaze traveled the same path around the living room as Ryan's, but her response was dramatically different. "Going somewhere?"

"Yes, actually. Venezuela." Even though I told myself that I didn't care what anyone thought, I held my breath and waited for their reactions.

"Wow," Pippa laughed. "Weird time to go on vacation, just after you left your job, but have a good time."

I smiled, truly happy to have Pippa back in town, she had a straight forward way about her. "Thanks, but it's not a vacation."

"Well, what the hell is it, then?" Ryan practically roared the question at me.

I glared up at my brother who the world thought was the quiet, soulful one of the group. "What the hell it is Ryan, is none of your damn business." I turned back to Pippa. "There's been some political and civil unrest in the country, and it looks as if they're heading for civil war. I'm going down there to cover the story for my new digital paper." Saying it like that, out loud and full of pride, felt good. I felt accomplished. Worthy.

"Wow," Pippa said again.

"It's a big step, I know that, but I have to do this. This is my chance to see if I have what it takes to be a serious journalist. And I don't care if you like it or not, Ryan. I'm doing it. This is my shot, and I'm taking it."

"You chose to stay," was his only response. "It was your choice to stay here, so don't blame me, or any of us for your choices."

"I don't. I blame myself and I blame Daddy." I shook my head in disgust. "I believed him when he told me that I would get to run the paper someday, that I would be able to choose the stories I wrote and published in the paper. Hell, that I was at least capable of choosing the layout." It had taken me far too long to realize the truth, and that was on me. "I believed that he was sincere in his promises, and yeah I was scared too, so it took me a little longer than it should have to leave."

"What about Stevie?" He asked in that smug tone that made me want to smack his face. "Or did you forget about her. Ouch, what was that for?"

Pippa glared up at him. "You're out of line and being an ass."

"Unlike you, my daughter is actually proud of me for chasing my dreams. So happy she's volunteered to speed the week with her father. She does have another fully functional adult parent you know." I felt angry that no one was supportive of me, and my shoulders sank with disappointment. "I'm not asking for your permission or your blessing, I'm just telling you that it's happening. The same way you three told me you were leaving Carson Creek and heading to Nashville to pursue your dreams. The only difference is that I was happy and supportive, sent you idiots cash when you needed it. I guess it was too much to expect the same in return."

"Does Daddy know?"

I turned my back on my brother and swiped at a furious tear as it slid down my cheek. "Leave Ryan, now."

"I'll take that as a no."

"Take it however you want, just take it out of my house."

"This is ridiculous Lacey. You're a mom and you're in your forties, what the hell is this?"

"Oh holy hell man, just get out," Pippa growled and gave him a shove. "Get out and don't come back until you can give your sister what she gave you guys when you were just starting out."

"But Pip," he began just as she gave him one final shove and slammed the door in his face.

She turned to me with a wide smile and her hands on her invisible hips. "You're going to Venezuela. How in the hell did this happen?"

"Levi," I admitted and told her the whole story. "He promised Michelle he'd be there for her and then passed the story on to me."

Pippa sighed. "So, this is a thing, you and Levi?"

I nodded. "It's been a secret thing for a while, but it doesn't have to be for much longer. He's a good man."

"I'm happy for you Lacey, but let's get down to the really important stuff. How's the sex?"

"So good I'm convinced I've been doing it wrong my whole life." My face fell into my hands as I giggled. "So good."

"Well Amen to that, sister." She held up a hand and I gave her a high-five in return. "You'll have to tell me everything when you get back from Venezuela. In one piece."

Yeah, that.

CHAPTER 22
LEVI

"Lacey."

Her name came out on a rough and ragged exhale the moment the door opened and my eyes took her in. She's dressed in cutoff jean shorts and a white t-shirt that molded over every single one of her curves, making my mouth water.

"Levi," she sighed, lips turned up into a seductive smile. With a glint in her eyes, one arm snaked out and grabbed a handful of my shirt before I was yanked inside. Lacey's smile was all I could see for a hot minute and then her lips crashed down on mine, a ferocious heat washed over me as all of those delectable curves pressed against the hardness of my body.

My hands went to her hips and gripped her tight before sliding down to cup her beautiful ass, to pull her closer to where I needed her most in that moment. Lacey moaned against me and jumped up to wrap her legs around my waist, bringing me right up against the fire between her thighs. "Lacey, babe."

She giggled when I swung our bodies around so she was pressed up against the door. "Now Levi, I need you now."

Our clothes came off in a frenzied rush, tossed in every direction in our eagerness, our need to get as close as possible as quickly as possible. The tiny shorts were so damn sexy I almost didn't want to peel them off her, but her legs came down so I could do just that. Her breaths came out short and jagged as I dragged the denim down her silky-smooth thighs as she stepped out of them. I inhaled her scent through the silky green fabric that covered her core. "Lacey," I growled a moment before I pressed a hot open mouth kiss right on top of the fabric.

"Yes, Levi." Her head fell against the door, her hands fisted in my hair while I feasted on her, licking and sucking until she flew apart on my tongue. My tongue slowed, but I didn't stop until I'd wrung the last ounce of pleasure from her body that I could. "Wow," she grinned down at me. "Making up for lost time?"

I laughed and stood, a growl escaped when her hands went straight to my waistband. "Making sure you don't forget about me while you're off on your grand adventure." I was only half-joking, but traveling was intoxicating, and this was Lacey's first big trip as a journalist. Even if she became addicted to it, I wanted her to remember what was waiting for her at home. And who.

"I definitely won't forget that feeling, or the man who made me feel that way," she shoved my jeans and boxers over my hips before she sank to her knees. "Someone is very happy to see me." Her eyes glittered with mischief as she stared up at me while she stroked my erection until it was so hard it ached. "Very happy."

"Almost as happy as I am to see you." She was beautiful, more so when she was having fun, and right now her skin was flushed with pleasure, her lips tugged into a smile.

"Well then," she said a moment before her lips parted and she took me in her mouth, using her wet tongue and lips to drive me crazy. Her hands gripped and squeezed my ass, and she took me so deep my eyes closed, one hand tangled in her hair and the other pounded the front door as she sucked me and dragged her tongue along my sac.

"Lacey." My eyes opened I looked down at her, my gaze slammed right into her smiling eyes and I smiled in return. "Fuck."

She moaned and the vibrations ricocheted through my whole body, shaking my spine as I tensed with imminent pleasure. She took me even deeper and moaned again.

My hips reared forward once before I took a step back. "Need you now," I growled and picked her up so that she was sandwiched between me and the door. We stared at each other for a long, hot moment and I thrust up into her wet core, her silken center hot as it clenched around me. "Yes."

"More," she begged as she wrapped her arms around me, nibbling my bottom lip, my jaw, my shoulder, giving just as much pleasure as she received. "Yes, Levi, oh yes!"

My hips thrust like a madman, sinking deeper and deeper as her body pulsed around me, so close to peak pleasure. Her hips moved against mine, thrusting down as much as she could while I devoured her mouth, her breasts, the sounds of her pleasure stirring my desire until I was on the brink of madness.

"Levi, don't stop," she moaned as her head thrashed back and forth against the door, her fingertips dug into my shoulders. "Please."

Her words, her highly charged pleas, tore me apart and I pressed my chest against hers, thrusting harder and deeper and faster until sweat dripped down my spine. Our mouths fused together in those last moments as pleasure struck, my body shook against hers, convulsing in pleasure. "Lacey," I growled against her lips and held her close. "I can't get enough of you."

"Ditto," she panted with a smile as she quivered one last time. "Damn that was...unreal."

"Felt pretty real to me."

Lacey laughed and shook her head. "So damn real."

Her words were like a kick in the chest, in the best

possible way. Or maybe it was my sex addled brain assigning more meaning to her words than she meant. "Lacey."

Her head fell against my neck and she turned her head as her tongue poked out and slid up and down my throat. Despite the intimate moment, we both laughed when her stomach growled impressively. "Good thing I brought lunch."

"The perfect man," she purred. "Brings me food and orgasms."

Her words wormed their way into my heart and settled deep as I gripped her ass and carried her to the living room. "Don't you forget it, babe."

She laughed and smiled down at me. Her body twitched as she sank down deeper on to my still pulsing erection. "Oh wow. Still?"

"What can I say, you do it for me." I wiggled my eyebrows and she laughed again, letting it trail off to a moan as I hardened inside of her.

"Levi," she moaned and rolled her hips, eyes lit with lust and need. Her gaze locked on mine and her hips sped up, moving in ever faster circles and strokes that quickly took her up to the peak.

She was gorgeous as she chased down her pleasure, beautiful breasts bouncing in my face, I couldn't look away just tasted her hard tips while she rode me until her head dropped forward, forehead pressed against mine.

"Oh, Levi," she moaned and moved faster still as breathless words of pleasure fell from her mouth. "So good," she hissed. "Yes." And then she gripped my shoulders and slammed down harder and harder until she froze and then shuddered as her body pulsed and clenched around me.

Her cries combined with watching her take her pleasure from me was more than enough to send me over the edge a second time. "Maybe I can be your cameraman," I joked and she rewarded me with a laugh.

"I am not opposed to that, or doing this at the end of every day." She shivered as our bodies separated and she fell against the sofa beside me. "Not opposed at all." Her satisfied sleepy grin hit me in the chest, and I pulled her close.

"Same," I sighed and dropped a kiss on her forehead.

After a luxurious shower that would have environmentalists protesting outside, we found our way to the kitchen to enjoy the lunch I'd gotten up early to make for us on this special day, our last together until she returned from her trip. "Oh my god Levi, did you really make all this?" Wide blue eyes looked from the Korean feast on the table to me, and then a smile lit her face.

"I did. I wanted us to have a memorable last day together."

She let out a feminine sigh that sent my pulse roaring through my veins. "It was already memorable, Levi. This one is for the memory bank." She stared at me like I was something special, and I luxuriated in that look for a good long time. "Are you sad that you're not the one going?"

Her question was as open as her eyes as she waited for an answer. "Not at all. I'm envious because this is your first major story, but I'm right where I need to be, and more importantly, you're doing exactly what you need to do right now." I could tell she was both excited and anxious over the trip.

"Thank you for saying that, Levi. Ow, hot!" She chewed the bite of kimchi as if it was on fire. "Spicy."

"Yeah, it is. I might have gone overboard with the chili flakes."

"Delicious though. I've never had it. What is it?"

"Kimchi, fermented spicy cabbage." I told her about all the dishes I'd prepared, and her smile grew wider. "And this is a spicy kimchi stew."

"Levi this is so much, it's all so great." She sighed and did that head tilt thing women did that made a man feel ten feet tall. "Your encouragement means the world to me Levi, and your culinary skills, well let's just say they are a gigantic bonus."

I smiled back at her. "You mean the world to me, Lacey." I leaned over the table and pressed my lips to hers in a short, affection kiss meant to punctuate my words. "And I have a going away present for you."

"I thought gave me that already." She laughed, her eyes sparkled with mischief.

"That was as much for me as it was for you. This is just for you." I handed her a few sheets of paper. "This is more of a physical gesture, but I also emailed it to you."

She stared down at the papers with a frown. "What is it?"

I laughed at her suspicion. "It is customary to open a gift before asking questions."

Her eyes bounced over the words and I enjoyed the surprise on her face while I ate. "Cassidy Smith? You mean little Cassie Smith?"

I laughed. "Not so little anymore, she's twenty-six."

Lacey looked back down, brows tugged down. "She's in college getting her early childhood education degree, using her GI benefits?" She rattled off a list of her Army medals and honors during Cassidy's two tours of duty. "Wow, she's incredible."

"I thought so too, and I thought it would be a great human interest profile piece for your news site. Feel free to credit my source, Mickey Branson."

Her eyes lit with humor. "Really?"

"Yep, told me she was a real-life superhero and my interest was piqued."

"You're giving me this story instead of CCDJ?"

I nodded. "Of course. I saw the page last night and it looks great, Lacey. Congratulations."

Her expression was one of satisfaction and pride. "Thanks, Levi." She got up and rounded the table before she settled in my lap, arms flung around my shoulders.

"Thanks. You officially won the award for best boyfriend ever."

My heart expanded at her words. "So, I'm your boyfriend now?"

She nodded. "Aren't you? Or do you want to stay my secret lover?"

"Nothing secret about the way I feel about you, Lace." One hand gripped her thigh and the other cupped her ribcage. "You're mine. Don't forget that while you're off with Carlton."

She giggled. "I looked him up, he's quite handsome." She laughed again and shook her head. "But I'm happy with the handsome man I've already got."

"I'm happy with you too." It was the best afternoon I'd spent with a woman, and when it was time to pick up Mickey, I was sad to see her go. "Be safe, and let me know how you're doing when you can."

"I will," she sighed softly. "I promise."

I kissed her long and hard at the door. "I'll hold you to that promise."

CHAPTER 23
LACEY

"We have a meeting today with Umberto Garcia, he's the opposition leader of the For The People movement. He's agreed to talk to us, but on his terms and his turf." Carlton had turned out to be a much better asset than I imagined. It wasn't just his fluent Spanish that helped, but the fact that the man seemed to know people everywhere. "It's a three-hour drive from the city."

I nodded as Carlton rattled off the details and sucked in a deep breath. Three days in Caracas had yielded a ton of content from the field that included interviews with current government officials, slice of life pieces with locals caught in the middle, and beautiful photos of this gorgeous country. "Garcia, he used to be a stock analyst right?"

"Yep. Left that behind after making a gazillion

dollars to hold government officials accountable for everything from broken campaign promises to corruption."

"All right, great. I have plenty of questions for him." I felt like I was back in college with all the research and cramming I'd done to formulate intelligent questions that would give me the answers I needed. It was tiring, but it was beyond exhilarating.

"Good. We should head out in the next fifteen minutes." Despite his easygoing spirit and laidback demeanor, Carlton was as serious as they came when he was in work mode. "Don't dress for the office. Jeans and boots, hiking boots if you brought 'em."

I nodded and dug the worn hiking boots from the bottom of my suitcase. "Okay, thanks." Carlton had advised not unpacking to ward off theft attempts, and to make it easier for a fast getaway if necessary.

"You're doing great Lacey. Stop worrying."

"I'm trying," I told him around a sigh. I was happy to be here, excited to see the city even if everyone was in a state of bated breath, waiting to see what would happen next. "I can't stop the anxiety."

"Good, it'll keep you alive."

"No pressure," I sighed and then laughed. "I'm okay. Good. Great."

Carlton's deep laugh echoed in the room. "You're fine, Lacey."

The drive was more than three hours, which gave me

and Carlton even more time to chat and get to know each other. "Have you been all over the world too?"

He nodded. "Trice, maybe more. It's a good life, but it's stressful as hell."

"But you've got plenty of awards to show for it, and tons of bylines. Must be rewarding." I could only dream of having such a storied career.

Carlton, for his part, was pretty nonchalant about the whole thing. "I just tell the stories, and if it helps people become aware of life outside their small cage, I'm satisfied. The awards are nice because it means I get first shot at tagging along with the best journalists." He quirked a grin as his big hands deftly handled the uneven terrain that took us to Umberto Garcia's compound in San Juan de los Morros. The main building was a one-story brick structure that blended into the forested wilderness around it. It was impressive, but not what I expected for a man worth millions of dollars.

"Wow, this place is incredible."

"And strategically situated," he added cynically. "Behind this place is where a national park starts, which is basically the wild."

I nodded absently for a long moment before we got out of the car and were approached by Garcia and two armed men. "Ms. Gregory. Mr. Linelli. Welcome to San Juan de los Morros." He smiled a picture-perfect politician's grin.

"Nice to meet you, Mr. Garcia." He wasn't at all what

I expected, dressed like a soldier instead of a businessman or a politician. In fatigues and combat boots, a big black automatic weapon was draped across his back, camouflage hat shielding his face from the oppressively bright sun. "This is quite a home you've got, beautiful and fully integrated into the natural landscape."

He smiled. "My wife would appreciate that sentiment if she were here, but shopping in London has taken her away for the foreseeable future."

More like he'd sent his family away to keep them safe from unrest and from his political enemies. "Lucky woman."

"Well, I have worked hard in my life to give my family every advantage." A perfect political answer if I ever heard one.

"Yes, and now you're a man of the people, doing what most men in your position would not."

He chuckled. "What is that?"

"Worry about the have-nots when you have so much."

"It is a sad state of the world when that is the fact, isn't it?" Umberto and his men led us to the back of the property where an oversized umbrella sat a few feet away from a bright and striped tent. "You can use the tent if you like to keep your equipment cool."

"Thanks." Carlton dipped inside while I took the chair about two feet from Mr. Garcia.

"So, why is it that you have so much concern for the

common man, Mr. Garcia?"

His smile came slowly. "I *am* the common man, and I was raised by a common man. What I learned in the upper echelons, if you will, is that the system has been rigged for the rich to stay rich, for the successful to become more successful."

"And you used that rigged system to get ahead?"

Garcia nodded vigorously and smiled at the camera over my shoulder. "Why should I not? But my plan is to get rid of those corrupt practices so that those who don't come from money and power can achieve it if they want." Garcia shook his head. "We deserve a better choice than the lesser of two evils."

The man was charismatic, and I could see clearly why the powers that be were concerned. A startled gasp escaped at the sound of machine gunfire in the distance.

Garcia smiled again. "It is disturbing, isn't it? That the government can just shoot at will against those who merely disagree with them? You see, they own the resources, they own the enforcers, and we are not allowed to get upset about the fact that we as a nation are not thriving. What sense does that make?"

"None," I agreed easily, still on edge about the gunfire that seemed to grow closer every few minutes. "But surely you have a plan beyond changing the laws? You still have a National Assembly to contend with."

"Free and fair elections are key, but there's another 'F' people leave out. Frequent. Let the people decide who they want to lead them. Government is a service, not a job program for rich people to keep the system rigged in their favor."

"So, your plan is to oust the entire government?"

"My plan was to convince these scoundrels to do the right thing. The current president didn't win the election, so how can we expect anything but corruption? This may not be palatable to your American sensibilities, but for us, this is the only way."

The gun fire was closer now, so close I could hear cries of agony as bullets hit flesh and blood people. "What's going on?"

Umberto glared at me and then Carlton. "You've led the opposition right to me?"

"Impossible," Carlton insisted. "We used the directions provided by your men that took us an extra hour to get here."

Umberto was terrified, and despite my own fear, I was happy to see that he was more than just a stuffed shirt. He knew the risks of his political speech, of his opposition, and still he persisted. "Grab them," he ordered his men and four more armed men appeared, grabbing me and Carlton and hurrying us towards a van that idled on the small service road between the compound and the national park.

I risked a look out the back window to see if it was police or military or a combination of both that had breached Umberto's property and aimed automatic weapons our way. "Who is that?" I turned over my shoulder to see Carlton beside me, camera lens aimed out the small window on the van's back doors.

"Those are our enemies, Ms. Gregory. See how they are dressed in all black with face coverings? No official insignia on the uniforms or vehicles? That's how the government works these days, and that is what I am trying to change."

I shook my head and sank to the floor of the utility van, body shaking with fear as the gunfire went on and on behind us. We drove over rough terrain, and I had no idea how long or how far we had driven. "They mean to kill you?"

"Most efficient way to get rid of me, but what they fail to understand is that my death will change nothing. There are thousands, possibly millions of Umberto Garcias who oppose them. They are just too set in their ways to see it."

I looked across the van at Carlton who had his camera aimed at Umberto's profile as he motioned for me to keep talking. "We're rolling," he mouthed. "It'll be saved to the cloud," he assured me.

I sucked in a deep breath and let it out slowly with my eyes closed in an effort to block out the nonstop gunfire. When I was sure my voice wouldn't shake, I turned to face Umberto and continued my interview.

Like a professional.

A terrified, out of her depths, professional.

CHAPTER 24
LEVI

The sound of the phone vibrating on my nightstand woke me up right away. I wasn't alarmed, it was just a habit from a lifetime of middle of the night phone calls that some part of the world was on fire, literally or figuratively. I reached for the phone without looking at the screen.

"This is Levi."

"Levi, it's Saul."

Those three words knocked away the rest of my sleep and I jackknifed up to a sitting position, eyes wide open in the pitch-black bedroom. "Saul. What's up?" Even before he answered, I knew what he was going to say. I *knew*.

He let out that same worried sigh I'd heard so many times over the years. "Lacey and Carlton, they're missing. We're coming up on the third check-in that's come and gone without a word."

"Shit." The word came out scratchy as I pinched the bridge of my nose. "What was the last news you heard?" I listened carefully as Saul caught me up.

"I talked to Lacey just before they left. She was excited and nervous about the trip." And now she was in trouble, lost and out of contact.

"Carlton hinted she might be important to you and since this is the first time in all the years I've known you that you handed off a story. I figured she must be very special, and I wanted you to know."

"Thanks Saul, I appreciate it. I'll pass the word on to her family." Shit, her family. Lacey's brothers were out of town and Stevie was with her father, which only left Pippa and GG.

"I'll keep you in the loop, and if you hear from them before I do..."

I nodded. "You'll be my first call."

"All right. I'm doing my thing," Saul assured me and ended the call.

I don't know how long I sat on the bed staring off into space, but I sat there with my feet hanging over the edge until they fell asleep. I shook my legs until the feeling returned, and then I moved into action. My first call was to Pippa.

"This better be good," she growled into the phone.

"It's Levi, and it's not good. I'm coming to pick you

up. I'll be there in five minutes."

Silence on the other end of the call lasted so long I thought she'd fallen asleep again. "All right. I'll be ready."

"Thanks." I ended the call and let out a long breath before I looked at the door. I'd stayed at Michelle's tonight since she was on the overnight shift for her surgical rounds. Well, the truth was that she was on the around-the-clock shift.

I had to wake Mickey and it was the middle of the night. He would be a cranky monster come tomorrow, but this had to be done. I crept to his room and went inside, watched his sleeping frame, so small, trusting and innocent. "Hey Buddy, we have to go out on a late-night adventure."

Mickey blinked up at me, a half-smile forming on his lips. "Adventure? Really?"

I nodded. "Yep. Grab your sweats and let's get going."

"All right!" And just like that, my grandson was on his feet and digging through his dirty hamper like a mad man, tossing clothes out over both shoulders.

"Hey Mickey, how about some clean sweats kiddo?"

"Oh. Yeah." He giggled as he walked quickly to his tiny race car themed dresser and pulled out a pair of sweatpants with a matching shirt. "Ready."

"All right kiddo, let's get going." I got Mickey settled in the backseat and headed towards Pippa's.

"Where are we going Grandpa?"

"I have to go talk to Lacey's family about some things."

He frowned form his car seat. "Is Lacey all right?"

"I don't know yet. She's been out of contact for a few days so right now let's just say she's okay."

"She is," he sang. "Miss Lacey is good at stuff."

She was, but nobody but the locals and guerrillas were strong enough to brave the wilds of Venezuela. Pippa was waiting on the porch when I pulled up to her place, brows furrowed and lips pinched in a tight line.

"What's going on Levi?"

"I'd rather not have to say this twice, but I need you to come to CCDJ offices with me. And I'm really sorry to wake you up so late, but I didn't know who else to call."

"I'm family, you did the right thing." She turned to offer Mickey a smile. "Hey Champ, how's it going?"

"Good, Miss Pippa. How's your baby?"

She smiled. "Still cooking. Should be ready in a week or two."

Mickey giggled again. "You can't cook a baby, you'll go to jail."

"Okay, well the baby is still growing and won't be coming out to meet us until all the baby growth is done." She turned back and sank against the seat. "Any day now, I hope."

Silence fell over the car except for the sound of Mickey humming to himself.

"Oh my goodness, I can't take it Levi. Tell me what's going on. Please."

"Wait until we get to CCDJ, GG will be there." The old man probably wouldn't take the news well, but my only concern was delivering the news.

"Lacey," she whispered softly. "Is she all right? Just nod or blink or something for yes or no."

I sighed and glanced back at Mickey who was suddenly very interested in our conversation. "Pippa," I began gently to keep the pregnant woman from freaking out. "She's not hurt as far as I know, and that's all you get."

That seemed to satisfy her for the few minutes it took to get to the newspaper offices. GG was inside Lacey's old office, bent over the layout table with a critical eye. "GG."

He looked up at me and then Pippa, and then Mickey. GG's spine stiffened and his gaze bounced over all three of us half a dozen times before a frown darkened his face. "What are you lot doing here? What's going on? Is it Ryan? Roman? Derek?"

My sad expression turned to anger, and I glared down at the stubborn old man. "How about your daughter GG, are you concerned about her at all?"

GG stood a little taller, and when he spoke his tone was filled with disbelief. "What the hell is wrong with Lacey?"

I took a deep breath and let it out slowly, hardly able

to believe the words that were about to come out of my mouth. "Lacey and a cameraman, Carlton, were interviewing the opposition leader a few hours ago outside Caracas. During the interview gunfire erupted and Lacey and Carlton were forced to flee into the national park with Umberto Garcia and his security detail."

"No," Pippa's hand flew to her mouth. "Seriously?"

I nodded, my expression grave as I said the words aloud. "Right now, we don't know who exactly was behind the gunfire, but the likely culprit is the current President. It's been thirty-six hours since they checked in with anyone."

GG's shoulders fell and he sank onto a nearby stool. "Shit, not my baby girl."

"Shit's a bad word," Mickey whispered with awe.

"Yeah it is," GG growled and pointed a finger at Mickey. "You should only say it in times like this when your little girl is missing in a foreign country."

Mickey frowned and went to GG, patting his knee. "It's okay, Miss Lacey is strong. She opened a jar once without any help from anyone, not even Grandpa." He whispered the words like they were a state secret, pulling a rough laugh from the old man.

"Thanks Mickey, you're right. She is strong. And brave."

"They might just be out of range," I assured everyone, including myself. "Hiding until the shooting stops."

"Or they could be lying dead in the jungle somewhere. Injured and mangled, hoping for help that never comes."

"Don't be mean mister." Mickey glared up at GG, a move that might have intimidated the old man from any male older than six years.

"There's no reason to think that yet, GG. If things weren't so up in the air, we would have heard. If nothing else, Venezuelan news sources would report on Garcia's demise. No news is hopeful news, so for now, let's all focus on that."

GG shook as his anger built. "This is your fault," he aimed a shaky finger right in my direction. "If not for you, she wouldn't have been so gung ho to run off, head first into danger."

I laughed. "Shows how much you know your daughter, old man. If you'd respect her more this might all be nothing more than a dream, one she's always had I might add."

GG scowled, disbelief written all over his face before he turned to Pippa, who gave a confirming nod as she stepped between the two of us and reached for Mickey's hand. "You two can take up this pissing contest later, right now we need to focus on Lacey and Carlton, sending them good vibes."

Mickey tugged on Pippa's hand, and she smiled down at my grandson. "What's a pissing contest Miss Pippa?"

She barked out a laugh. "It's when two men argue

unnecessarily about something neither of them can change, placing the blame on the other to relieve them both of guilt."

"Oh. Okay."

There was one other matter, and given my lack of skills as a father, I turned to Pippa. "Does Stevie need to know yet?"

"No. I don't want her to worry unless we know something definitively, or it ends up on television."

"How in the hell are we going to find out anything *definitive?*" GG growled at Pippa. "She's thousands of miles away, and no one knows where she is."

Pippa pointed an accusing finger at GG. "Stop it. Right now, GG."

The two bickered like old friends and I pulled out my phone as a thought occurred to me. I checked Lacey's website to see if she'd been able to upload anything that she was unable to publish. "Whoa, wait! Shut up," I told them, voice elevated over their shouts. "A story just published to her site not even ten minutes ago.

It was Lacey in the back of a windowless van, a man armed with an automatic rifle sat behind the driver as the vehicle bounced over uneven terrain.

"We don't know where we're headed," she said directly to the camera. "Umberto and his men are officially on the run from unknown sources who have been shooting at us for more than an hour." The video cut to a small square window behind Lacey, revealing two pickup trucks and a hummer

with men dressed in black, hanging out the windows. They were the source of the gunfire. Lacey turned back to Umberto. "Who do you believe these men to be Mr. Garcia?"

"My enemies," he said plainly. "They are practically in uniform, but where is the insignia? Local or national law enforcement? Who knows? My guess is the current so-called leader of our great country."

"They would do that?" Lacey's question was asked simply and with the appropriate amount of shock for American viewers.

Umberto nodded. "Absolutely. I would not be the first opposition leader to disappear or die under suspicious circumstances."

Lacey swallowed visibly as the sound of the gunshots grew louder and nodded. "And that doesn't worry you?"

"Of course it does. I have a wife and children who care for me. I have employees who rely on me to feed their families. But even if I am dead today, tomorrow someone else will take up the fight."

The distinct sound of bullets hitting the metal van sounded followed by Lacey's terrified scream. Carlton's arm reached out to grab Lacey and shove her to the ground. Seconds later, the screen went black, and gunshots sounded for a few seconds more.

"Wow." Despite her fear, Lacey powered through the interview. I was so damn proud of her. So happy for her.

"She's crazy, completely crazy, and it's all your fault Levi."

"You're kidding?" I asked in a shocked tone that shouldn't be so shocked at all by his words. "She's done it, GG. The one thing she wanted to do most in her career, and she didn't falter, she thrived. She got the information she needed, she told the story, and thanks to her news site we know that. Something you have refused her for a long time."

"She's in danger."

"Sure, and if she hates me when she gets back, I'll deal with that. But you? She could have done this on and off over the years, but the story would have been over by the time she returned to Carson Creek to put it in the newspaper. She's damn good at what she does and you're holding her back, and if you don't get your head out of your ass, you're going to lose her forever." I reached out for Mickey. "Come on kiddo, let's get out of here."

And if they didn't find a way to safety, I might lose her before I got a chance to tell her how much she means to me.

"Grandpa, how do you get your head in your ass?"

I laughed. "It's just a saying Mickey. It means you're not thinking straight."

"You mean like forgetting Miss Pippa?"

Yeah. Just like that. I stopped and turned to find Pippa with her arms folded as she stared at me and Mickey halfway down the stairs. "Yeah, kiddo, something like that."

CHAPTER 25
LACEY

"It's a good thing you told me to wear hiking boots," I joked to Carlton as the sun hit its peak on day four. Four long days in one of the national forests of Venezuela and I was exhausted and scared as hell. I didn't sleep much at night or during the day, every snapped twig and flap of a bird's wing made me jump out of my skin. The one thing that doesn't suck is Umberto's cabin which is the most luxurious cabin I've ever seen. There's indoor plumbing, so I got to drink filtered water every day, which more than made up for rationing food among five adults. There were three beds which weren't cots and I happily slept head to foot with Carlton who I couldn't stop thanking for saving my life.

Carlton laughed at my hiking boots comment and raised his camera. "I just hope that this incident hasn't soured you on this type of journalism." His dark eyes were sincere as he waited for my answer.

I smacked at my left bicep that now sported four bug bites and looked around at the beautiful scenery. The *Aristides Rojas* was breathtaking, and the B-roll footage Carlton had captured so far was perfect for a nature documentary. So far, we had walked the forest on each side of the building, never straying far enough that we couldn't see the cabin.

"Are you kidding me? Despite, or maybe *in spite,* of the gunshots and hiding out in the forest, I've never been so scared and excited at the same time in my life. Imagine that your ideas are so revolutionary that the government wants to take your life." I knew it happened, of course I knew that. You don't make it to your mid-forties by being childishly naïve, but it was still unbelievable. I held my hand up when the camera turned my way. "Don't record me," I chided him because I hadn't showered since the morning we left the hotel, my hair was a mess and my clothes were filthy. I wasn't a vain woman, but I did have standards.

"Why not? We might be up here a while, and I think we might as well get as many eyeballs on this story as possible, especially since Umberto has satellite out here." Carlton lifted one broad shoulder casually. "Might help us get rescued by someone who doesn't want to kill us."

"Good point," I sighed and dropped my hands from

my face because Carlton was absolutely right. As terrified and anxious as I was, this was a once in a lifetime story, and I had exclusive access. I shook out my stiff limbs, stretched the muscles in my face and finger-combed my hair. "Okay."

"You look good Lacey. I mean you look good for a woman who's been lost in the jungle for four days."

"Thanks," I told him and glared at his laughing face.

"The question I wonder most about in all of this madness? If the government is threatened because Umberto is right, and his ideas threaten their very existence, or is it because his ideas are just that dangerous?" I stared into the camera and shrugged. "Everyone who seeks to lead a country is convinced their ideas are right, are the best ideas for the people, but sometimes they are not."

Leaves crackled on the ground behind me just as Umberto's deep voice spoke. "Governments and power," he began, holding up three large fish from a rope in one hand. "The government, any government is a machine, one that exists for the sole purpose of maintaining the status quo. The organization is more important than any one individual. These days it seems to be the other way around."

I nodded because that shift seemed to be happening more and more around the world. "You think these officials aren't in the government to serve the people?"

Umberto laughed, a deep and rich laugh that made

him even more likeable. "They sought out positions of power that allowed them to keep the system rigged for them and for people like them."

"You understand how hard it will be for people to believe you, a very wealthy man, mean those sentiments?"

Umberto nodded. "Of course, but I worked hard to become successful. I didn't have any advantages until I was already a success." He smiled at me, mischief in his eyes. "Ever cleaned a fish before, Ms. Gregory?"

I nodded, happy to do something that would make me forget I was on camera. "You can call me Lacey, and I've cleaned and gutted more fish than I care to admit."

"Excellent," Umberto laughed. "It is refreshing to see a beautiful woman unafraid to get her hands dirty."

I laughed off his compliment and walk to the mudroom that was already lined with newspaper. "I'm a Tennessee girl, fishing is how you impress boys, spend time with daddy and rustle up a quick, cheap meal."

"You still live in Tennessee?"

"Yep. Born and raised. I left for college and came back."

"Me too," he answered with a smile. "No matter where you go, home is where you belong. The people here don't care about my success, they are proud of a hometown boy succeeding, but they'd rather have my smarts making the country better than just offering a handout."

"I find most people are like that, but everyone loves to focus on those who want nothing but a handout. Why do you think that is?"

"It riles up the masses and gets them to support legislation that goes against their best interests. And that gives the government what they need to keep lining the pockets of their designer pants."

We talked about governments and power structures until the fish was ready to cook, Carlton unobtrusively filming it all. At the end of the interview, I smiled at Umberto. "Okay Mr. Man Of The People, let's see how well you can fry up a fish."

He pointed a finger at me, his expression teasing. "I will surprise you once again Lacey."

When Umberto disappeared into the house, Carlton smiled. "That was great. You're a natural."

"I guess we'll see when this interview goes live." Never in my life had I been so grateful for my compulsive need to keep my laptop charger with the laptop wherever I went. Carson Creek Online would still exist when I got back home.

If I got back home.

CHAPTER 26
LEVI

"Mr. GG, where are the comics?" Mickey spent the past few afternoons in the CCDJ offices because keeping track of Lacey through Carson Creek Online, while maintaining my duties for the paper as well as profiles and articles for The Old Country House had kept me plenty busy.

"Comics aren't for papers," GG grunted with a smile. Mickey had stolen his heart just like every other person the boy had ever met. "You want comics you buy a comic book."

Mickey giggled. "I like comic books."

"Of course you do," GG grumbled to himself, still smiling.

"Grandpa, look!"

I turned just in time to see a video of Lacey and Umberto Garcia playing on network television. Before I could find the remote to crank up the volume, my phone rang and Saul's name flashed on the screen. "What's up Saul?"

"Your girl is incredible, Levi. She is the real deal. Have you seen the most recent footage she sent, of her and Garcia cleaning and gutting fish together while talking world politics? Good shit, man. Very good shit."

His talked on, all the while my gaze remained fixed on Lacey on the television. She was beautiful and mussed, smiling and laughing at whatever the charming rebel was saying.

"I'm sorry what?"

Saul's deep laugh turned into a cough. "That woman is a natural. With that hint of country accent, her fresh face, and the fact that she's beautiful and intelligent? I'm tempted to poach her from her small town."

And from me. I growled and Saul laughed at me.

"Now I see exactly why you don't want to come back to civilization. I wouldn't come back either."

"She is part of it, but not the only part." Mickey and GG were both looking up at the television. At Lacey. "What else?"

"I looked over the footage she sent last night, and it has some good information in it, including the exact national park, which is still near thirty square kilometers. There are Army guys nearby and ready to perform ex-fil as soon as their location has been pinpointed."

"That's good news, Saul. Really good news. Thanks."

"I should be thanking you for sending me a gorgeous woman who can talk world events while gutting a fish. That's gotta be one of those fetish videos or something, especially if you throw in the twang." Saul laughed again, the way he did when he knew he had something good in his hands.

"Happy to return the favor after all these years." Saul had sent me on some of the most exciting and terrifying trips of my career, giving me first bite at every war, every conflict, coup and inauguration around the world. He was one of the main reasons I'd had the career I did. "How are the numbers on this story?"

"Through the roof. The American people are paying attention, especially after this last interview that's been playing on a loop since midnight, gunfire in the distance."

"I'm going to check Carson Creek Online."

"No need," Saul shouted. "It's not going to be able to handle the capacity, so do what you can for her until she gets back."

I smiled at the way he was already so protective of Lacey. "I'll take care of it, not until after I spread the word that she's all right." If the town hadn't already heard about it. "Thanks again, Saul. For everything."

"No thanks necessary. One day I'm going to ask you both to jump on a plane and cover a story together and you're going to say yes."

I laughed and ended the call, wondering if that trip

would come sooner rather than later. And then another thought came to me, a selfish stupid thought that made me feel like the world's worst boyfriend. Lacey's career was on the way up, if that's what she wanted, and mine was here in Carson Creek with Mickey and Michelle. Would I now be on the receiving end of the life I'd inflicted on my ex and my daughter for decades?

That was a rough thought, and a selfish one I was ashamed to admit to out loud.

"Good news?" I looked up and found GG eyeing me warily. "About my little girl?"

"Somewhat." I passed on Saul's information to GG with the hope that it would activate the gossip chain in town so I wouldn't have to. "Ready to go Mickey?"

The little boy nodded. "I'm hungry Grandpa."

"All right, go get your things." I stood and stretched my back, feeling my shoulders a little less stressed than they had been when I woke up this morning. "Are you going to be all right GG?"

"Now that I know the good ol' U.S. Army is looking for my little girl? Yeah, I'm fine. You?"

"I'll be better when she's back here." In my arms.

"You and me both." GG waved me off. "Go on and feed little Mickey. He's got a ton of energy for a starving child."

I laughed. "Tell me about it. See you in the morning. I'll call if I have any information."

"Yeah, thanks."

Mickey and I made our way home where a big pot of steak chili was bubbling in the slow cooker waiting for us. The front door flew open as soon as my key turned in the door, and Michelle stood there with wide eyes and a shocked expression on her face. "Dad, oh my god you haven't said a thing!" She wrapped her arms around me and pulled me inside. "Lacey," she sighed. "I saw her on TV."

I returned the hug with all the energy I could muster. The news about Lacey had zapped some of my strength, or maybe it was that I could finally breathe a little easier knowing there was a plan in place, that she was all right. "She's okay, and the Army is involved now."

"Oh good," she sighed and bent down to give Mickey a hug. She stood and studied my face for a long moment. "You don't look happy about it."

"I'm thrilled, actually. But I'm also worried that with her new exposure, I'm about to get hit with a heaping dose of karma."

She laughed. "I doubt it. Lacey loves her home and her daughter, she might go out a few times a year, but she'll stay here more than she'll go away, and that's only if she wants to risk all *this* again," Michelle said and waved absently at the TV. "There's also the other thing."

I frowned and closed the door. "What thing?"

"I'm hungry," Mickey whined, and we all headed towards the mouth-watering scent that wafted from the kitchen.

"Go wash your hands," Michelle ordered with a grin and turned to me. "You can tell her that you love her and give her another reason to stay."

I dropped down on a chair with a sigh. "That was the plan, but now that I've seen the footage, I can't do that to her."

Michelle rolled her eyes. "Dad you're not doing anything *to* her, you're giving her your heart. Your big ol', totally in love heart. This is for her as much as for you."

I shook my head because that was the last thing I wanted to be for her, another reason to abandon her dreams. "I can't."

Michelle scoffed and handed me a beer from the fridge, a move that formed another ball of regret in my stomach, that I'd missed this during the years when she might've tried to steal a sip or two. "You can, and you will Dad. She deserves to know that you love her, that she is loved, especially after all she's been through. Let her know that she has more than Stevie to come home to from her next trip."

"I'll think about it."

"No, you'll tell her. Let her know you're proud of her and that you love her as soon as you have her in your arms. Trust me on this."

"Okay, I will," I conceded easily, because I wanted Lacey to know how I felt, and I also wanted her to know that I would wait for her.

CHAPTER 27
LACEY

My eyes were closed as I listened to the sounds all around me. A constant beeping sound that never seemed to fade or grow tired, a whirring noise that I couldn't figure out, and shuffling feet just outside my door. It was, clearly, the sounds of a hospital and I opened one eye and then the other. My gaze landed on the spray foam of the ceiling, lined with fluorescent lights. A long, curved rod held the ugliest floral curtain I'd ever seen, meant to offer me a modicum of privacy in a place not built for it. A quick glance to my right revealed a table with a cup of ice and a pitcher. To my left, the source of all the noises I couldn't identify.

I looked down and wiggled my toes, moved my legs and then my fingers, my arms and my head. *Everything is working properly.* That was a good sign, so I tried to sit up and look around, to orient myself once again, because every day that I woke up for the past three days, I went through this routine because I was sure I'd wake up in Umberto's cabin.

Again.

The door opened and a nurse I knew from middle and high school, Shelby, shuffled in with a smile. "Good morning Lacey, how are we feeling today?"

I raised a hand in greeting. "I'm still exhausted and a little dehydrated. Still a little paranoid, but I'm alive and safe and healthy."

She smiled. "That's great to hear. You ready to get out of here today?"

I nodded and sat up again, this time successfully. "Is that really going to happen?"

"Yes. The doctor says you'll continue to heal, but you no longer need constant monitoring. If anything worsens, come back to see us, all right?" Shelby grinned. "Can I just say that you were incredible during all that hullabaloo. You kept your cool, you looked great, and you told one hell of a story."

"Uh, thank you Shelby." I hadn't gotten much feedback that I could remember other than from Carlton. I had done two interviews with major news networks who were dying to be the first one to tell my story. "I was just trying to not think about everything else."

"Well, I never watch the news, too depressing ya

know? But I was glued to this whole thing. It was just riveting." Shelby shivered. "Anyway, I'm just glad you're all right. Those bug bites are gonna sting like the dickens for a few more days. No scratching," she admonished, "or you'll have scars everywhere. Call if you have any questions."

"I will," I assured her. "I promise." With a smile and a nod, Shelby left me to my thoughts, which mostly centered around seeing Levi for the first time in weeks. Would the same spark be there? Would he be jealous that the story had turned into an international sensation, or would he be the proud, handsome man that had kissed me goodbye and wished me luck?

I didn't have any answers, so I spent five minutes just breathing deeply the way Carlton, the undercover yoga lover, had showed me when the nights got longer and quieter, and the gunshots drew closer and louder. The beeping noises sped up and then slowed as I got my breathing under control. Pippa would arrive within the hour to coincide with the time Shelby said I would be discharged if things all went according to plan. I couldn't wait to see Pippa, though I couldn't deny my disappointment that my brothers and my father weren't coming. Stevie, I knew, would have some small celebration planned for the two of us.

But Levi had been suspiciously absent and quiet.

Oh well. I would figure out what, if anything, was going on with us when the time was right. The first thing I wanted, and desperately needed, was the hottest shower I could tolerate.

Forty-five minutes later a knock sounded on my door, and then it opened to reveal the smiling face of my beautiful daughter. "Mom! Oh my god, you're here! You're alive." Stevie rushed over and flung herself on top of me in a melodramatic fashion befitting her age. "I'm so glad you're okay."

One hand stroked her hair and the other patted her back as a few sobs shook her slender frame. "I'm fine sweetie. I have about ten thousand bug bites, but otherwise, I'm good. I'm home."

"Good." Stevie pulled back and wiped her eyes. "Because you were like, totally awesome out there. Your voice barely shook when those jerks with guns were chasing you. So badass."

"Language," I admonished automatically and without much heat. "But thank you." I reached for her my daughter and hugged her again, as tight as I could, because there were so many hours I wasn't sure if I'd ever get to hold her or scold her again. "I missed you, Stevie."

"I missed you too Mom. But I'm so proud of you. You were so brave, and all the boys at school think you're a total hottie." She rolled her eyes, disgust mixed with pride shining in her eyes. "Even Dad was impressed."

"High praise, I suppose."

"And best of all? Shannon was so green with envy I thought she might just keel over."

I couldn't help it, a laugh bubbled up out of me and I shook my head. I didn't have any animosity towards Shannon, but I could admit—to myself—that it felt good to have her be the one feeling a hint of jealousy. "How did you get up here?"

"I brought her." Levi appeared in the doorway like a big sexy lumberjack, complete with days old scruff that added to his rugged air. His expression was tight with a tension I couldn't quite read, but a moment later his feet were on the move, crossing the room where he scooped me in his arms and held me close for several long moments. "I'm so damn happy to see you, and touch you, and know for myself that you're all right."

I laughed at his concern. "Levi, you are a sight for sore eyes." I squeezed him back and allowed my body to lean into his, let him take some of my weight while I soaked up his scent and his feel. "Thank you," I whispered in his ear. "Thank you Levi, for giving me the experience of a lifetime."

"Yeah? You don't hate me for sending you off to run from government henchmen?"

"Hate you? Never." That was another thing I'd realized with too much time to think, that my feelings for Levi went much deeper than I allowed myself to admit. Now wasn't the time to tell him, but soon. "I'm grateful. Truly."

Levi's shoulders sank in relief and his honey brown eyes studied me, took in every detail, as if he was cataloguing the difference since he'd seen me last. "I am so proud of you Lacey. You were great out there, calm and cool with dynamite questions. And best of all? You looked hot as hell out in the jungle with a fish in one hand and a knife in the other. Like a country girl fantasy with a dash of Christiane Amanpour."

His words touched me to my core. Okay, maybe I swooned at bit at his romantic, sweet as sweet tea words. Then again, maybe I was still feeling a bit weak and dehydrated. And then I laughed. "That is the sweetest and the oddest compliment anyone has ever given me."

"That's me," he said with a sultry smile as he leaned in until I could see the threads of gold in his brown eyes. "Sweet and weird." Levi smacked a kiss against my mouth and we both ignored the gagging sounds Stevie made from the other side of the room. "Now go get out of those sweats, your adoring public is waiting."

I pulled back with a frown and blinked rapidly. "What are you talking about?"

Stevie crossed the room and shoved a bag in my arms. "I brought the necessities for you to make yourself human again. We have a surprise for you Mom, so let's get moving." She clapped her hands with a purpose, the same way I had seen her do when she was leading her squad in a routine.

"Brat," I murmured under my breath.

"I heard that," Stevie shot back, a smile in her voice.

I rolled my eyes and gave Levi one last lingering look before I stood up and made my way to the bathroom to do as my daughter instructed. To make myself human again. Inside the bag I found my face wash, moisturizer, body lotion, a hairbrush, and the perfume I tended to wear most often.

I had to laugh at the clothes Stevie had chosen, a spaghetti strap sundress that hit just below the knees, the perfect dress to show off the great majority of my bug bites. I was hoping to look a little sexier when I saw Levi, but he'd already seen me in sweats with hospital bed hair, so this was a big step up I suppose.

I primped until I looked as good as I could, took a deep breath before I stepped out like the badass I felt like.

And promptly took Levi's breath away.

CHAPTER 28
LEVI

She was gorgeous.

Stunning as she stepped out of the hospital bathroom looking like a million bucks. Her bruises and bug bites were hardly noticeable in the bright yellow dress with large pink and white flowers that made her look like the sunshine that lit up the sky. Her sun-kissed skin highlighted the freckles on her shoulders, and it all worked to make her sexy waves look like a golden halo around her head.

"Damn Lacey, you look beautiful."

She blushed prettily like it was the first compliment she'd ever gotten. "Thank you, Levi." Lacey glanced around the room and sighed. "What about this surprise you were telling me about?"

I laughed and glanced at Stevie. "Did we say that?"

Lacey arched a brow and folded her arms, tempting

me to talk. "Pretty sure you both are plotting something."

"Come on superstar, let's get out of here." Stevie and I grabbed her things and headed to the car while Lacey received aftercare instructions from the nurse and an overwhelming farewell by the staff.

"She looks uncomfortable," Stevie commented as we leaned against the car watching Lacey from the pick-up bay.

"She'll get used to it," I assured the girl.

I felt Stevie's gaze on me, her eyes serious and assessing. "Did you?"

"No," I admitted. "I tell the stories, I'm not part of them. But in this instance, your mom is the storyteller *and* a character in the story." The more I watched Lacey, the clearer it became that she felt trapped by all the attention and praise. "I'll be right back."

"Her hero," Stevie called after me in a sing-song voice that made me smile.

"Sorry ladies, we have to get the patient home to rest and hydrate." I flashed my most charming smile and wrapped a possessive arm around Lacey, enjoying the way she leaned into me as if relieved I was there. "Thank you for taking such good care of Lacey."

The nurses smiled and tittered as they waved of us. "Wish I had a man like that of my own," one nurse said loudly. "Does he have any brothers Lacey?"

She shook her head, arms wrapped around mine as we walked out of the hospital. "That was a lot."

I put one of her hands to my lips, brushing a soft kiss across her knuckles. "You're a star now Lacey, and everyone wants to know you."

She huffed. "Take me home. Please."

"Gladly." I pressed a kiss to her lips before we all piled into my car and headed for Lacey's house. The drive was mostly silent, each of us lost in our own thoughts. My mind was full of thoughts of Lacey, swinging from happiness and relief that she was home safe, to fear and anxiety of what I had to do today. Share my feelings.

It was the last thing in the world I wanted to do, but Michelle has cajoled and chided, and literally twisted my arm to make sure today was the day I told Lacey, in no uncertain terms, how I felt about her. If I could find the courage. And the words.

Lacey gasped beside me as we turned onto her block, the streets lined with cars, balloons, streamers and signs welcoming her home, congratulating her on her success, and telling her they were all proud of her.

"What's all this?"

"Your adoring public Mom. Duh." Stevie jumped out from the back seat with so much energy, I wondered if I could bottle and sell it.

I turned to Lacey. "You heard her, let's go meet your adoring public."

She sighed. "This isn't the public, these are people I've known for years."

"That's why it means so much. They know you, know who you are and what you're capable of. More than that, they were genuinely worried about you. Like I was."

"I'm fine," she insisted.

I speared my fingers through her soft, flowing waves. "And I for one, am so happy see that for myself. I was so scared, Lacey."

"Me too." The soft, whispered words touched me deeply, and warmth exploded in my chest.

"I wasn't sure I'd ever get to see you again, and the thought of that laid me low Lacey. I never want to be without you again." My hands cupped her face and I brought my forehead to hers. "Not ever."

"I don't think you'll have to worry about that anytime soon," she assured me with a hint of humor.

"You say that now, but once things have returned to normal, once you've written up the story in its entirety, you'll feel differently." After that rush of adrenaline and fear faded, the need to pursue exciting stories like that only increased.

She pulled back and stared at me, confusion swimming in her eyes. "Why do you sound upset about that?"

I sighed, trying for a smile that felt weak even to me. "Because Lacey..."

She nodded and put more space between us.

"Because you're not as okay with it as you said you were?"

My brows dipped and I reached for her hands, pulling her back to me. "No, that's not it at all."

"Yeah?" She asked bitterly, fire now replaced the confusion. "Then what is it? Is this the, *it's not you, it's me* speech?"

"No." I smiled, her anger was sexy as hell, especially when I knew something she didn't. "It's not that at all."

"Then what is it Levi? I'm feeling really confused right now, and I don't like it at all." She paused for a second and turned towards the passenger door. "Maybe we should have this conversation later."

"No." I pressed the automatic lock button, risking her wrath. "We need to talk now. I've been waiting a long time, probably too damn long, to have this conversation."

"Fine. What conversation?"

I sighed and clasped our hands together palm to palm. "The conversation where I tell you that I've fallen in love with you."

She blinked once. Twice. Three times. Then, she let out a heavy sigh and my own pulse kicked up, wondering if I'd gotten this all wrong. "Levi," she whispered.

Aw, hell, I had gotten it wrong. "I messed up, didn't I? This was only ever a secret love affair to you." Despite her best boyfriend declaration, it wasn't that serious for her.

"No, you didn't mess up Levi. You just...shocked the hell out of me."

I laughed. "You? I'm the one who had to get those words out."

Her smile was bright and beautiful. "You mean it, Levi?"

"Yeah, I mean it. Absolutely. Totally and completely." I shouldn't have waited to tell her. "I realized when I got word that you were missing, I realized that waiting might have meant you died without knowing that you were loved. That I would never get the chance to tell you how I feel about you."

Lacey freed one hand from mine and cupped my face. "I'm glad you got the chance to tell me Levi. But I have to ask, why does being in love with me seem to upset you?"

I shook my head. "It doesn't upset me at all, I'm just wondering if telling you this now is fair to you. To both of us, really."

"What does fair have to do with it?"

I laughed. "Because Lacey, whether you want it or not, you're famous now, and more than that, you're popular. A brave and beautiful woman telling an incredible story the way you did? You'll have offers lining up to send you all over the world to do that again and again."

She frowned. "I want that for you sweetheart, more than

anything. I'm so proud of the videos and stories you've already put up, and I can't wait for what comes next in your career."

"And you think it's not fair to you?"

"No," I laughed again and shook my head. "If you accept every single offer put in front of you and leave me behind to wonder when you'd be back for any length of time, that would be karma. No less than what I deserve. I think it's not fair to you."

Lacey shook her head, wisps of curls flying around her face. "Okay, you're going to have to explain this to me because I don't understand."

"I don't want to tell you I love you in an effort to convince you stay in Carson Creek. I want you to go out and experience everything you never got to before now, I just, I need you to know that Lacey."

Her shoulders fell. "You love me enough to push me to the far flung corners of the world?"

I blinked, and thought about how she'd phrased it. "Yeah. Exactly. I love you, and I want to spend as much time with you as I can, but I also want you to go out and conquer the world on your own terms. You deserve that."

"You sweet man," she whispered and pressed her lips to mine. "I don't want you to worry about keeping me here, Levi."

"Because nothing can keep you here?"

She laughed, and the sound was melodic and feminine. "No, because this town is my home—for better or for worse—and I will always come back to Carson Creek. I'll always come back to you too, Levi."

I held my breath. "Yeah?"

"It would be really inconvenient to fall in love with a guy and then never come back home to him, because that's what you've become to me Levi. Home."

Home. That sounded nice. Really nice. "Say it again."

"So bossy," she murmured and shook her head. "It's a good thing I love you, bossy thing that you are."

"I love you too Lacey. With my whole heart." I couldn't wait another minute to wrap her in my arms and I rushed out of the car, jogging around the front to pull her out, flush against me, so all of her soft curves were smashed against mine. "So damn much," I growled and then I kissed her because she was home and she was safe, right here in my arms. Most of all, she was mine.

All mine.

CHAPTER 29
LACEY

There were so many people in my house. So. Many. People. Carson Creek wasn't one of those small towns with a population of five hundred, but it was small enough that everyone knew everyone.

Or so I thought.

As I looked around at the familiar faces like Ryan and Pippa, my other brothers Roman and Derek, Valona, Trey and their three girls, I was struck with how many strangers there were in attendance. At my house. Carlotta stood by a man I didn't recognize, who looked at her like she was his everything. Even Margot and Jared had come to welcome me back, both with men I didn't recognize.

But they'd all showed up to see me, to congratulate me on my big break. At forty-five. I wore a smile and accepted all the kind words for as long as I could stand it, but the truth was, all the praise made me feel as if this one story was my sole accomplishment in life.

"Hey, what's wrong?" Levi flung an arm around my shoulders and whispered the question in my ear, punctuating it with a nip of my earlobe.

"Nothing, it's just, you'd think I didn't do anything until this moment. I ran a newspaper for the past twenty years, raised a wonderful daughter, but this is my only claim to fame?"

"Or maybe they're just happy you've finally gotten to go out and chase another of your dreams. Your brother Ryan has always been a writer, but now he's writing songs for other artists and people are excited for that new opportunity. Same thing with Roman. It's no different Lacey." He kissed my cheek and wrapped me in a hug that made me forget everything and everyone else around us.

"Get a room," Ryan said and bumped Levi out of the way to pull me in for a hug. "So glad you're safe, big sis." His gaze fell on Pippa, who I was sure had forced him to come make peace with me.

"Thanks," I grumbled against his chest. "Even though you were totally against me going in the first place."

"I was worried about you, rightfully so," he shot back with a sheepish smile. "But I'm glad you're home, and I'm so damn proud of you, Lacey." He squeezed me in a bear hug that stole my breath.

"Thanks, Ryan." His words meant a lot to me, but as Levi's words played in my head, I let my anger go. It didn't matter what Ryan or GG thought of my choices, all that mattered was that I was proud of myself and setting a good example for my daughter. "I appreciate it."

"So, we're cool?"

"Yeah sure, we're good." He was my brother, and I would love him always, but my choices were mine. Good or bad.

"What about us?" GG's voice grumbled behind us and practically sucked all of the energy from the room. "Are we all right?"

I turned around and tried for a smile, but GG looked older than the last time I saw him. Greyer and thinner, like a man his age. "Daddy," I sighed. "Sure, we're fine."

"Fine," he grumbled and stared at me for so long I thought he'd fallen asleep with his eyes open, and standing. "I've been alive long enough to know that when a woman says 'fine' it means anything but." His assessing gaze never wavered, and I sighed.

"Why wouldn't we be fine? Just because we don't work together, doesn't mean you're not still my daddy. Right?" I held my breath, because I really didn't know what his answer would be.

"You'll always be my little girl Lacey. Even when

you're being stubborn and brave, running through the wilds of a foreign country."

"That's good to hear Daddy."

"I'm proud of you Lacey."

Fireworks exploded in the pit of my stomach at his words, the same words I'd waited a lifetime to hear. They were important, but there wasn't that sense of relief I thought there would be at hearing them. "Thank you, Daddy."

"I guess that means you're done with the paper for good?" I couldn't tell if he thought it was a good thing or not.

I shrugged. "You don't need me, and I'm happy where I am now."

He nodded slowly. "I thought as much. My loss, I suppose, for not appreciating a good thing when I had it."

It was on the tip of my tongue to offer to help out, but Levi was there behind me, a strong presence to remind me that I wasn't just GG's daughter, I was a grown woman. A journalist in my own right. Instead my lips tugged into a grin and I pulled him in for a hug. "Let's do lunch together soon Daddy, just you and me."

He smiled brightly in return. "I'd like that a whole lot, honey." Daddy squeezed me back, and in that moment I knew we would be all right. I might never work at CCDJ again, but our relationship would be fine. Maybe better than fine without the back and forth of us arguing over every little detail of the newspaper.

"Me too," I told him and took a step back, suddenly very happy Stevie and Levi had put this party together for me at the last minute. These were my people and this was my town, the place that had nurtured me from a little rough and tumble Tennessee girl, to a grown a woman, a mother, a divorcee, and now a semi-famous reporter. They'd always been here for me, and they always would be, and I absolutely loved them for it.

GG nodded gruffly and walked away, the same as he always was, yet also completely different.

"That was weird," Ryan said, breaking the silence in our small circle. "I thought for sure he'd have a smartass comment."

"He's probably saving it up for tomorrow," I assured my brother with a smile. "Or maybe everyone has grown up but you, Ryan."

He held a pretend dagger to his chest and stumbled backwards. "You wound me, Lacey."

I rolled my eyes at his antics and smiled. "You're so lucky Pippa, your baby will already have another kid to play with from day one."

"Lucky me," she sighed and grabbed Ryan with an affectionate smile. "But he's got big arms to carry plenty of food," she called after her shoulder and made her way to the long table stacked with food, brought by everyone in attendance.

"This is great," I told Levi honestly. "Really. I can't believe you guys were able to pull it together so fast."

"Had to do something other than sit at your side and stare at you until you woke up."

His admission put a smile on my face. "You were worried about me."

"Forever and always," he growled in reply, his gaze serious, and seriously sexy.

"I'm gonna hold you to that," I teased with a flirtatious grin.

Levi held me tighter and rested his chin in the curve of my neck. "I hope that's not all you're going to hold me to," he growled and pressed his body, his growing hardness into me.

"Is it too early to disappear from my own party?" I needed him. Badly. I wanted him right here and right now.

"I'm not up to date on my party etiquette, so let's just say it is never too early for a mid-party orgasm."

I turned to face him and wrapped my arms around him. "I love you Levi and I really love the way you think." My body molded to his and a low purr escaped right there in the middle of my very crowded living room.

"Yeah? Because I haven't been able to stop thinking about you pressed up against the bathroom door, biting your lip while I drive you out of your mind. Quietly. Very, very quietly."

A slow smile crept across my face. "Have I told you how much I love the way you think?"

Levi laughed and let his hands wander down to my ass for just a brief second. "I'll never get sick of hearing it," he whispered. "Do another round of smiling and shaking hands, and meet me upstairs in five minutes." He walked away casually, heading up the stairs as if he'd always been a part of my life.

I managed to smile and shake a few more hands, and I made it upstairs in three minutes.

To my man.

To my new life.

My new reality.

∼

THE END

PREVIEW: MIDLIFE FAKE OUT

She was the one with the bottomless brown eyes that always seemed to be on the verge of tears that never fell.

Those eyes had called upon all of my protective instincts.

But that had been too much responsibility for a high school boy.

I hadn't wanted or needed that kind of responsibility.

So I'd rebelled against those instincts, and did the opposite of protecting her.

I bullied her.

PROLOGUE

Derek – 2 Months Ago

A buzzing sound started to my left, and I flipped over to get the hell away from it. I didn't know what time it was, but the fact that I was still sleeping after the most epic awards show after-party meant it was too damn early for phone calls. But the buzzing didn't stop, and worst of all, there was a cold spot on my bed where a really hot model should have been. My eyes snapped open and I pushed off the bed, scanning the room for any trace of Sasha, or Satya, or something equally as trendy.

"Hello?"

Silence met me as the phone continued to ring. The bedroom floor no longer held a pair of tiny panties. Sheer tiny panties, if I recalled correctly, and I usually did recall, because I wasn't the kind of guy to forget what type of lingerie I tore off with my teeth. Names and jobs? Sure. To call? Almost certainly. But never lingerie. Ever.

I hurried out of the bedroom and down the hall where my black slacks sprawled across the top three steps. I distinctly remembered a long green dress with sparkles on it being somewhere near the bottom of the staircase, but now it was gone too. So were the sky high heels that capped off the longest set of legs I had ever seen. I went left at the bottom of the staircase, and the coffee table still held a half-empty bottle of champagne, two glasses beside it, one stained with a red lipstick imprint. My jacket was on the back of the sofa, along with the bowtie I'd left to hang around my bare chest, because that's what people expected of Derek Gregory, the heartbreaker of The Gregory Brothers trio. Ryan was the moody and sensitive songwriter, and Roman, as the youngest, was the goofball bad boy. We all had our roles, and I'd played mine perfectly for decades now.

I retraced my steps towards the kitchen, which was of course empty, because everyone knew models didn't eat. But there was a note. I smiled and strolled over to the counter.

"Thanks for a good time, Derek. You more than lived up to the hype. *Xoxo – Sascha.*"

I smiled even wider because she was a perfect woman. Looking for a good time with no strings and no expectations, and gone before the awkward morning after, where I would have to explain that I wasn't looking for anything serious, while a woman stared at me with tears swimming in her eyes.

"So did you Sascha, so did you."

In the big empty Nashville mansion, the only sound was my stupid phone still buzzing upstairs on my nightstand.

I took the stairs two at a time, wondering if Ryan or Roman had found themselves in the wrong type of trouble, which rarely happened, but rarely wasn't never. I quickened my steps at the thought that it could be something wrong with our father, GG, or worse, our sister Lacey, who recently decided to become an investigative journalist covering stories in chaotic regions of the world.

"Yeah, what is it?"

A familiar sigh sounded down the line, and I pinched the bridge of my nose a moment before my agent, Brody's angry voice sounded. "So you haven't been abducted by aliens or models, and you're not lying dead on the side of the road," he grumbled. "I guess I should thank the lord for tiny favors. Very tiny."

I rolled my eyes because I knew that tone. "What did I do now?" Usually I managed to balance the line between lovable bad boy and asshole perfectly, but sometimes I stepped over that line. Sometimes I jumped over it by a mile. "Well?"

"You mean other than offending our core audience

with some attempt at comedy that just came off as sexism and misogyny? Is that not enough for you, Derek?"

"You're going to have to give me more details, because all I did last night was accept a few awards, dance all night, and made Sascha moan my name until the wee hours of the morning. So tell me Brody, how have I offended our beloved fans?"

"Stop me when this starts to sound familiar yeah? *She needs to be barefoot and pregnant soon, so you can get her back in the kitchen where she belongs.*"

I froze at those very familiar words. "Yeah they're familiar. I sent that exact text to my new brother-in-law. Yesterday. Was my phone hacked? Don't worry I don't keep nudes on there," I assured him with a laugh.

"Derek," he roared over the phone. "You idiot, you beautiful, talented fucking idiot. You didn't send that to your brother in law, you sent it out to your ten million followers."

"Ten? Try twenty-three million, not that I've been counting." I tried to be active on social media, to keep the fans engaged with photos of me and my brothers, me just living my life.

"Even worse. You did hear the words I just read back do you, didn't you? Barefoot and pregnant? In the kitchen where she belongs? To our mostly female fanbase!"

"Brody it's not that big of a deal. I'll explain that it

was a private message and a joke. I'll even do a video with my sister to show them." This will blow over in a day or two, it always did.

"No you won't. I don't want you to do a goddamn thing Derek, except what I tell you to do. What I need for you to do is go away. Just for a little while. Lay low and go on a social media hiatus until I tell you otherwise."

"What? You've got to be kidding me, Brody. It was just a joke!"

"It was the wrong type of joke at the wrong time, and it offended *everyone*! Go back to that Podunk town you're from and keep a low profile, Derek. Can you do that? For the sake of your career, and if not yours, then your brothers."

"Shit, you're serious."

"Yeah Derek, I'm serious. This whole situation is serious, and I need you to take it seriously."

I worked too hard on my career to lose it now over some silly joke. "I'm listening. Go home and stay away from the spotlight." My shoulders fell in disappointment. "Anything else?"

"No," he sighed in relief. "I need to get with the public relations team and figure out how in the hell to fix this mess. Don't do anything until you hear from me. Got it?"

"Got it."

There must have been something in my tone, because when Brody spoke next, his tone had softened.

"This isn't the end of the world Derek, but it will take some finesse to handle it. Just sit tight, and for once in your life, do as you're told. Tell me you can do that."

"I can do that Brody. My career means everything to me, you know that."

"I do, but I also know you're a stubborn asshole when you want to be."

"I'll close up the house now and head to Carson Creek today," I told him, completely defeated.

"Good. And stay away from all press and social media for the next few days, will you?"

I nodded even though he couldn't see me and dropped down onto my bed. Either that or my legs gave out as the gravity of the situation settled on my shoulders.

"Yeah, okay. Sure." I ended the call and sat on my bed for what felt like forever, contemplating how in the hell I'd ended up here after such a spectacular night.

We'd won three awards last night for our last album, including Song of the Year, and today here I was.

Exiled.

CHAPTER 1
BELLA

Early mornings were my favorite time of day, always had been. The world was quiet and peaceful as the earth tilted to meet the sun's golden rays, and only a few brave souls were awake to see the first beauty of the day. It was, and had always been a private time, a time for me to gather my thoughts and prepare for the day ahead.

Now that I was officially a farmer—again—of my own free will this time, early mornings and to do lists were a necessity. For now I was a one woman operation with the help of a barely teenage boy, who was now, technically, my son.

It hurt to think about Nicola's premature death. She was my best friend, my sister in all but the biological sense, and now she was gone thanks to that unforgiving bitch known as cancer. Her death had left me and her son Everest alone in the world, forced to cope without her sunny disposition and ability to see the positive in any situation. Now it was just us, two cynics who still hadn't found a way to do more than exist without her.

That's what Carson Creek was for. It was meant to be a change, a reset for both of us, but more of a homecoming for me. I grew up here in this town and on this farm. I tilled and watered the land, fed the animals, plucked the crops and sold them all over the state. I loved farm life, it was in my blood, and I'd always dreamed of taking over the place once Ma and Pa retired. Then high school started, and the bullying, the name calling, the stares and the pointing. What fifteen year old girl didn't want to wear makeup and look pretty for hormonal teenage boys, right? Even worse than my distinct lack of desire to impress said boys, my sister would argue that I went out of my way to make sure they weren't interested, but the truth was you could only wash your hands so many times to get the dirt from under your nails. Too many hours in the barn, and not even two showers could completely shake the smell of hay. And what was so wrong with the scent of hay anyway? Without it we wouldn't have food and nourishment, but that only made me more of an outcast.

So instead of sticking around and taking over York Farm, I hightailed it out of this town as fast as I could and claimed the college scholarship that waited for me in Texas, where I'd met my best friend, Nicola.

And now she's gone.

My phone beeped and the screen lit up to remind me that quiet time was over. "Ev, breakfast is ready!" I called upstairs to the sleeping teenager, because I'd learn one month into our first nine months together that yelling was more effective than a gentle shake to wake him from his slumber. The boy slept like the dead, a skill I envied each and every day. I waited and stared at the ceiling until movement stirred above me, before I finished my coffee.

Ten minutes later Everest made his appearance. At just thirteen, he was already the same height as me. But he was at that stage where his limbs were the size of a grown man's, but he was still very much a boy, with long gangly limbs, thick shaggy black hair that looked like it hadn't seen a comb in six months, and skin as smooth and as clear as a baby's. His mother's gray eyes stared back at me, and I couldn't help but smile at the heartbreaker in training.

"You're staring again, Aunt Bella."

"Yeah, I know, and I'm not sorry at all. I was just thinking that one day soon you're going to be such a handsome stinker." He already had the makings of it, and when his growth spurt hit and his baby fat melted away, young adult women of the world would lose their minds.

Everest smirked back at me, a blush stained his cheeks. "Yeah? What am I *now*, chopped liver?"

"Nah, I wouldn't say that. Right now you're a cute stinker, emphasis on stinker. Hungry?"

"Always," he laughed and grabbed the coffee pot.

"Still too young for this," I reminded him.

Everest shrugged and poked his head into the fridge where he emerged with a bottle of orange juice. "Better?"

"Water would be better, but that is acceptable."

"Water isn't going to give me the energy I need for a long day working the fields." It was a good attempt at a guilt trip, but it wasn't good enough.

I laughed and put one hand on my hip. "Working the fields? Hardly, more like feeding some animals and cleaning some stalls, which shouldn't take more than a few hours. When you're done you can go into town and see about making some friends." We'd been in Carson Creek for a few months now, and he'd barely left the farm or made an effort to mingle with the other teens in the area.

His shoulders stiffened at my words. "I don't need to make any friends, Aunt Bella. I'm fine here on the farm. I like it here."

I nodded, because I understood the urge to hide in the face of grief. "This is your home, Ev. You will always belong here, and that won't change if you go out and make a few friends. Have a little fun."

"Not yet, Aunt B. Okay?"

I nodded. "Okay, not yet then. But soon. You don't

want to start school as the new kid."

"Fall is months away. I'll be fine."

"Okay fine. If you'd rather spend time with your super cool aunt, instead of swimming with girls at the lake or sneaking beers at the movie theater, who am I to argue?" I laughed when he rolled his eyes, enjoying this time together, because I knew that one day soon, he would wake up and view me as the enemy.

"You know if this whole farming thing doesn't work out you might have a second career as a standup comic."

"Har-har. Thanks for the vote of confidence, kiddo." I pressed a kiss to his cheek and ruffled his hair before I grabbed my phone and headed towards the back door. "I'll be fixing the fence on the south end for most of the morning, and I have my phone. Take yours with you, just in case." I called instructions over my shoulder for what felt like the hundredth time, and then I was gone, out in the already warm and sunny day.

I smiled as I hopped in my shiny blue pickup truck and headed to the fence that probably hadn't been fixed since the last York left the farm about ten years ago. It was good to be back on the farm, this time around I was older, and supposedly wiser. I didn't need to make friends or connections for my social development, I'd given up on love well before the ink dried on my second divorce, which meant I only had to do two things in this world, raise Everest into a good man, and make this farm a success again.

Both jobs were daunting, and I wasn't even sure I had it in me to do either one of them well, but those were the only things I wanted to do, which meant failure was not an option.

I had a plan. For York Farm and for Everest.

The farm was the easier task to tackle, so I focused on that while I grabbed pliers and twisted the wire around the wood posts, replacing as necessary. The land was big by family farm standards, but there was enough room to grow squash, soybeans and tomatoes on the main plots. Eggs from the chickens would sell well, because they always did, and if the trees on the west end of the property were still good, maybe apples and cider in the fall. The vertical farming buildings were already producing, so the farm could start making a profit sooner rather than later, which would help replenish the money I'd spent to fix this place up and make it livable for me and Everest.

I had a stack of parenting books in my nightstand drawer. Admittedly, that wasn't the most exciting thing to have in that particular drawer, but the books were a greater necessity than battery operated lovers. I now realized that audio books might have been better, since most of my time was spent outdoors, and that way I could multi-task, learn the best ways to parent a child who'd lost his mother, while catching up on my never-ending to-do list.

Mending the farm fence was a hell of a lot easier

than the other fence I would have to mend someday. I wasn't much of a fence-mender in the real world, more of a fence burner. Hell, even that wasn't accurate. The truth was that I was more of a barn burner, I didn't just burn the bridge, I blew up the entire structure. It was my modus operandi because life was easier to deal with that way. Scorched earth meant there was nothing to return to, or attempt to fix later.

"What a joke," I muttered as I examined my handiwork. The fence looked good, but it was the only fence likely to actually get mended. At some point in the future, before I die, I would have to reach out to my four siblings, Abel, Amara, Andora and Alex, and do something or say something. Maybe an apology or something, I didn't have a clue what would do the trick, which meant it wasn't important enough to make it onto my to-do list.

Yet.

Everest likely needed more family than just me, and I had family members in abundance. Maybe the York family could be for him what they had never been for me. Or maybe I just hadn't given them a chance.

I guess my family would go on the list sooner rather than later.

Some days being the adult, the logical and reasonable one, really sucked.

CHAPTER 2
DEREK

It hadn't taken long for boredom to set in once I got back to Carson's Creek. I lasted one week staying with Ryan and Pippa. They were disgustingly in love and I was happy for them, but I didn't need to see my brother and sister-in-law making out while trying to enjoy my morning coffee. And my niece Ryanna was as cute as they came, but she was curious as hell, and when she couldn't explore she proved to have Gregory lungs.

Roman's place was empty, so I stayed there for a few nights since I'd sold my house in Carson Creek last year. That was a good decision at the time, since I didn't spend much time in my hometown, and when I did, I had three siblings and an ornery father to stay with. But my current stay in Carson's Creek wasn't quite working out as I had hoped. After one too many eager groupies showed up at my baby brother's door, I knew my social media restriction wouldn't last long.

So I did what any reasonably wealthy and completely exiled rock star would do.

I bought a farm. Or was it a ranch? It was a giant plot of land with several smaller buildings on it that I hadn't bothered to look into as carefully as my business manager would have liked. It was out on the outskirts of town, which made it perfect in terms of privacy, and there was enough room that I could probably turn one of the buildings into a studio. This exile might be the perfect time to start building my credentials as a producer, at least that's what I told myself, but seven weeks in, and I hadn't even called a contractor. Or hired anyone to tend to the overgrowth which was out of this world.

I thought about asking my neighbors next door, since the rumor in town was that someone had actually purchased or rented the York Farm, but I hadn't seen any evidence of their existence beyond a shiny truck and crops growing day by day. *Great, they were actual farmers,* which probably meant early to bed and early to rise.

The neighborly thing, the southern thing to do, would be to go over there and introduce myself. Maybe offer some muscle once in a while and hope they would do the same for me.

Another time, maybe. I needed, no, I wanted to get the studio built as soon as possible. It would give me something to do, and it would keep me out of trouble until Brody reached out to say I could make trouble again, and do it publicly. I got up and dumped my lukewarm coffee down the sink, I then went about my daily ritual of discreetly checking the internet to see if the women of the world still hated me, and—yep—they did. Instead of stewing over it and cursing the world for my bad luck, I headed outside, determined to scope out the perfect studio space.

The building closest to the main house would be ideal for convenience, but I could put in a small unpaved path if one of the other buildings proved better suited. It was so quiet that I could hear mosquitoes whizzing by my ears, birds chirping in the distance, even the crunch of overgrown foliage under my boots.

It was too quiet.

But I heard a vehicle in the distance, close enough that it was either a visitor for me, or someone at the York Farm was out and about.

My phone beeped with a message from Roman. *"Where the hell are you?"*

"I'm at home. Grounded."

That's exactly what it felt like. I was back to being fourteen and forced to sit in my room and do nothing, not one damn thing, because I'd gotten caught doing something stupid. *Some things don't change*, I thought and smiled to myself.

"We're here," was the next message that came through.

I made my way back to the front of the main house, an act that took even longer than walking the property of my Nashville mansion. Both of my brothers stood on the front porch looking around at the property, probably wondering what in the hell I was thinking.

"Hey, what are you guys doing here?" Not that I wasn't happy to see them, but I hadn't had any visitors in weeks. "Didn't even know you were in town," I told Roman.

Ryan shrugged and ran a hand through his long blond hair with a sheepish smile. "Pippa thought you might be going nuts out here by yourself and made me come."

"Gee, thanks man." I snorted and punched his shoulder.

"I would've come out if you had asked, but you're not exactly the begging type." He wasn't wrong. I didn't need a group to amuse myself, at least that's what I told myself, but I had been going a little stir-crazy out here on my own.

Roman shrugged and clapped me on the back with a playful smile as he gestured to the land before us. "I just wanted to lay eyes on the old hovel, see what kind of dumbass trouble you got yourself into now."

"It's hardly a hovel," I told him and shoved my elbow into his side. "The place just needs some tender loving care, which I plan to give it. With the help of a landscaper and a contractor." Even as I said the words, a vision of what the place would look like came to me.

"A contractor?" Ryan's arched brows nearly disappeared into his hairline. "For what exactly?"

I nodded for them to follow me around to the back of the house. "Afraid I'm going to open up a place to rival Dark Horse?"

"Hell no," he growled. "Nina is happy where she is, so anyone you could get would be a poor imitation."

I rolled my eyes. Nina was a damn fine chef and woman, but I had no desire to run a restaurant. "I'm going to turn one of the buildings into a studio, produce more tracks, maybe some albums for other artists. What do you think?" My brothers and I were close, very close, but we weren't the touchy feely sort to talk about our feelings until our voices went hoarse.

Ryan grinned. "Yeah? That's a good idea. Plus, the main house is big enough if you want to put the artists up yourself."

I hadn't thought about that, but it wasn't a bad idea. "Like those old artist communes back in the day," I mused, suddenly liking the idea more and more.

Roman snorted. "Of course you would decide to do this after my first album is done and on the shelves. But it's a good idea, a good way to keep busy until your current shit storm blows over."

"Don't remind me," I grunted. "One little mistake

and I'm being tarred and feathered." I still couldn't believe it, and I was pissed off. But I promised Brody I would be smart and that I would listen. "Anyway..." I said in search of a change of topic and coming up empty.

"Meet the new neighbors yet?" Ryan asked with a smirk.

"Nope. I guess they're real farmers or something." I did think it was strange that I hadn't even caught a glimpse of them yet. "Or vampires, possibly ghosts."

Ryan rolled his eyes. "Pippa was right, you are going crazy."

"Maybe the ghost farmers are just good at hiding from the misogynistic rock star," Roman mused and pointed to a figure off in the distance.

I followed the direction of his finger and let out a small gasp, because it was an actual person. "Unbelievable." I guess I had started to believe the place might be empty. Carson Creek specialized in gossip, but they didn't always get it right.

"Let's go introduce ourselves," Roman said and started towards the fence before anyone else had agreed. Typical youngest kid, always did whatever the hell he wanted.

"I guess we're going to meet the neighbors," Ryan said with a knowing smile that normally would have set me on edge, but nothing in my life was normal right now and it was all because of social media.

No, it was my fault. Plain and simple.

By the time we got to the fence Roman had already introduced himself, though it probably wasn't necessary because the kid already knew him.

"Oh wow. I love The Gregory Brothers, but your new album is incredible. Been listening to it on a loop since it came out," the teenager with black floppy hair had an awestruck grin.

Roman stood a little taller at the compliment. "I would offer a signed CD, but I wouldn't even know where in the hell, um heck, to get a CD anymore. But I'll definitely get something to you."

The kid laughed and shrugged. "You don't have to do that."

"You kidding? Without fans I wouldn't be shit, I mean hell," he sighed and scrubbed a hand over his face. "You know what I mean right kid?"

"Yeah," he nodded. "I do. The name is Everest, by the way." He finally noticed me and then Ryan with wide gray eyes. "Holy shit, do you guys live next door?"

"I do," I told him and stepped forward with a handshake. "I'm Derek, and I just bought the place. Haven't seen anyone next door at all."

Everest nodded and glanced at the property with a critical eye. "What are you planning to do with the land?"

"My first plan is to get the land cleaned up so I can see what my options are, but I'm going to turn one of the buildings into a recording studio."

"Cool," he nodded and looked around. "I can help clear the land if you want."

"Yeah?" I didn't know, given the current state of things, if that was such a good idea. "Why?"

He shrugged. "My aunt keeps talking about going into town and making friends. If I have something else to do, especially a job, she might lay off awhile longer."

I frowned. "You don't want to make friends?" What kind of teenager didn't want friends, especially a good looking kid like him that could easily be very popular?

"I just got here, and things have been rough. My mom passed away, and I'm just taking it easy for a while." He scanned the grounds once again and turned to me with those gray eyes that looked as if they'd seen too much. "I spotted some peach trees on the south end of your property, if you're interested in tending them, they look to be bearing fruit." The way the kid breezed over the dead mom information called to me, I'd done the same when we lost our mother.

I smiled at his mature way of speaking. "You grew up on a farm?"

"Nah, but my aunt did, and she knows all kinds of stuff."

"So why aren't you helping her?" Roman shoved his hands in his pockets and leveled Everest with a look.

"She only lets me feed the animals and clean their living areas because she wants to make sure she can handle the workload when I become the most popular kid in town." He snorted his opinion at that aspiration. "Anyway, you know where I'll be if you decide you want some help. It's a big job."

We all smirked at how easy the kid was with us. "Everest, why did you guys choose Carson Creek?" There were bigger towns and bigger farms throughout the state.

He shrugged at first, and then lifted his eyes to the blue sky and blinding sun. "She grew up here. Said she didn't much like it here back then, but that it was a great place for us both to start over, so here we are. Oh and this is her family's farm."

No. it couldn't be. The universe couldn't be so cruel to me, not now when I was exiled to my hometown. The universe would not trap me beside my biggest regret, would it?

There were five York kids, and three of them were girls. It could just as easily be Andora or Amara, but my gut knew that it wasn't. It was the svelte York sister, the one with the bottomless brown eyes that always seemed to be on the verge of tears that never fell. Those eyes had called upon all of my protective instincts. But that had been too much responsibility for a high school boy. I hadn't wanted or needed that kind of responsibility. So I'd rebelled against those instincts, and did the opposite of protecting her.

I had bullied her. Badly.

"One of the York girls," Ryan mused. "Which one?"

"Bella York," a rich feminine voice answered as she

came to a stop beside Everest. She was as beautiful as ever. Gorgeous with her long limbs, strong and lean. Her white tank top showed off her shoulders and toned arms, a pink bra peeked from behind one of the straps. But her legs were the real superstars, encased in denim that looked damn near painted on. A floppy hat sat on top of her thick brown hair that hung halfway down her back, or would have if the wind hadn't picked it up and swirled it around her body. She put a hand on Everest's shoulder and smiled. "The Gregory Brothers. Hey Ryan. Roman." She didn't say my name or even look in my direction, and I wasn't at all surprised.

"Bella York," Roman purred and leaned in with an appreciative smile. "You always were a pretty thing, but holy hell woman. I'm of legal age now," he reminded her and wiggled his eyebrows.

Bella laughed, and the sound was thick and rich. "Thanks Roman. And congratulations on your solo and group success. You guys are all over the place."

"We took a risk, and it paid off." Ryan shrugged like it was no big deal. "What are you planning to grow?"

"Quite a bit actually. Soybeans will be our biggest crop, there will also be squash and tomatoes, and hopefully some apples from the orchard. I also have a vertical farm with plenty of herbs and leafy greens. A lot of stuff," she said with an embarrassed laugh. "Sorry."

"Don't be," Ryan assured her. "I own Dark Horse, it's

a high end restaurant in town, and my chef Nina loves to come out and pick fresh food. She would love this."

I watched as she chatted easily with my brothers, and wondered to myself how it was possible that she had gotten even prettier over the years. She was still willowy with this innately delicate look about her, but now there was also a strength about her, inside and out. "It was great to see you guys, a real blast from the past. But I need to get back to it," she said and thumbed in the direction over her shoulder. "Tell your chef to come by anytime to check the place out. I'm happy to show her around." She took a few steps back, brown eyes smiling wide at my brothers before she turned to Everest with an affectionate smile.

"What about me?" I shouldn't have said anything. I should have just left it well enough alone. She didn't like me, probably hated me, and she had good reason to ignore me completely. But that just wasn't my style.

Annabella York froze and turned slowly to level me with an icy glare. "What about you?"

I took a step forward and licked my lips. "Am I welcome anytime?"

She flashed a sexy smile, and I swore my knees gave out a little. She was hot as hell fully clothed, and I couldn't help but imagine what she would look like in nothing at all.

"You, Derek Gregory are welcome, never. Not ever, even if there's an end of the world disaster. Unless of course you have a fondness for the taste and feel of shotgun slugs."

"Ouch," Roman groaned and then laughed.

With a pointed look at me to make sure I got the hint, she turned and walked away, long legs eating up the space quickly.

My brothers roared with laughter at her insult, looking at me with questions in their eyes that I refused to answer. "I can't wait to hear that story," Ryan said around a loud guffaw.

Even Everest laughed. "Wow. I'm pretty sure Aunt Bella hates you, and she likes everyone. *Everyone*," he emphasized. "Sorry," he added with a shrug. "It was nice to meet you guys. All of you." He waved and walked off, shaking his head with an amused smile.

As soon as Everest was out of earshot, Roman laughed even more loudly. "What the hell was that about man?"

"Ancient history," I growled and walked away from the fence, putting as much distance between me and Bella York as possible. With her so close, her hatred so palpable, it didn't feel all that ancient. It just felt like another thing that I would have to apologize for.

Eventually.

Some day.

Later.

Bella & Derek's story continues in Midlife Fake Out.

Also by Piper Sullivan

Midlife Fake Out: Bella & Derek

Midlife Love Story: Carlotta & Chase

Midlife Love Affair: Lacy & Levi

Midlife Valentine: Valona & Trey

Midlife Do Over: Pippa & Ryan

Healing Love

Dueling Drs, Book 6: Zola & Drew

Rockstar Baby Daddy, Book 5: Susie & Gavin

Unfriending the Dr, Book 4: Persy & Ryan

Kissing the Dr, Book 3: Megan & Casey

Loving the Nurse, Book 2: Gus & Antonio

Falling for the Dr, Book 1: Teddy & Cal

Curvy Girl Dating Agency

Forever Curves, Book 8: Brenna & Grant

Small Town Curves, Book 7: Shannon & Miles
Curvy Valentine Match, Book 6: Mara & Xander
Misbehaving Curves, Book 5: Joss & Ben
Curves for the Single Dad, Book 4: Tara & Chris
His Curvy Best Friend, Book 3: Sophie & Stone
Curvy Girl's Secret, Book 2: Olive & Liam
His Curvy Enemy, Book 1: Eva & Oliver

Small Town Protectors (Tulip Series)

That Hot Night, Book 12: Janey & Rafe
To Catch A Player, Book 11: Reece & Jackson
Cold Hearted Love, Book 10: Ginger & Tyson
Hero Boss, Book 9: Stevie & Scott
Dr's Orders, Book 8: Maxine & Derek
Mastering Her Curves, Book 7: Mikki & Nate
Kissing My Best Friend, Book 6: Bo & Jase
Undesired, Book 5: Hope & Will
Wanting Ms Wrong, Book 4: Audrey & Walker
Loving My Enemy, Book 3: Elka & Antonio
Bad Boy Benefits, Book 2: Penny & Ry
Hero In My Bed, Book 1: Nina & Preston

Accidental Hookups

Accidentally Hitched, Book 1: Viviana & Nash

Accidentally Wed, Book 2: Maddie & Zeke

Accidentally Bound, Book 3: Trish & Mason

Accidentally Wifed, Book 4: Magenta & Davis

Boardroom Games

His Takeover: An Enemies to Lovers Romance (Boardroom Games Book 1)

Sinful Takeover: An Enemies to Lovers Romance (Boardroom Games Book 2)

Naughty Takeover: An Enemies to Lovers Romance (Boardroom Games 3)

Boxsets & Collections

Small Town Misters: A Small Town Protectors Boxset

Misters of Pleasure: A Small Town Protectors Boxset

Misters of Love: A Small Town Romance Boxset

Misters of Passion: A Small Town Romance Boxset

Kiss Me, Love Me: An Alpha Male Romance Boxset

Accidentally On Purpose: A Marriage Mistake Boxset

Daddies & Nannies: A Contemporary Romance Boxset

Cowboys & Bosses: A Contemporary Romance Boxset

About the Author

Piper Sullivan is an old school romantic who enjoys reading romantic stories as much as she enjoys writing them.

She spends her time day-dreaming of dashing heroes and the feisty women they love.

Visit Piper's website www.pipersullivan.com

Join Piper's Newsletter for quirky commentary, new romance releases, freebies and contests.

Check her out on BookBub

Stalk her on Facebook

Printed in Dunstable, United Kingdom